COLTON 911:

# AGENT BY HER SIDE

## DEBORAH FLETCHER MELLO

## ◆ HARLEQUIN
# ROMANTIC SUSPENSE

### Danger. Passion. Drama.

*These heart-racing page-turners will keep you guessing to the very end. Experience the thrill of unexpected plot twists and irresistible chemistry.*

**AVAILABLE THIS MONTH**

**COLTON 911: AGENT BY HER SIDE**
DEBORAH FLETCHER MELLO

**FAMILY IN THE CROSSHAIRS**
JANE GODMAN

**COLTON STORM WARNING**
JUSTINE DAVIS

**GUARDING HIS MIDNIGHT WITNESS**
ANNA J. STEWART

ISBN-13: 978-1-335-62672-1

50575

▷ EAN

HRSATMIFC1020

## Cooper took a step and Kiely grabbed the back of his jacket.

The look she gave him spoke volumes. She understood him wanting to rush in, but they needed to proceed cautiously. They didn't want anyone to get hurt, most especially his little boy. Until they could assess who and how many people were inside, they needed to stand down.

Cooper nodded his understanding, inhaling deeply to quell his anxiety. Moving swiftly, they approached the home prudently. Kiely took cover behind a tree as Cooper took the steps, his weapon drawn. Inside, the child suddenly cried out as if in pain. His little scream was gut-wrenching, even to Kiely. Evidently unable to contain himself a moment longer, Cooper became less an agent and more a father as he rushed the door, Kiely covering his back.

Shots, fired from the inside and through the front entrance, sounded one after the other.

*Bang!*

*Bang!*

*Bang!*

All three shots splintered the wood door and hit Cooper square in the chest. The blows sent him backward down the stairs as Kiely screamed his name.

\* \* \*

**Colton 911: Grand Rapids**

**Where there's danger—and true love—around every corner...**

\* \* \*

**If you're on Twitter, tell us what you think of Harlequin Romantic Suspense!**
**#harlequinromsuspense**

Dear Reader,

There truly aren't enough words to express how much I have enjoyed joining the Colton author family. Being asked to participate in the 911 continuity series was a dream come true. I found breathing life into Cooper and Kiely's story to be so much fun! These two are fire and fire, and I love how their love story came together. Their all-or-nothing approach to life is only tamed by their parental responsibilities to Cooper's baby boy, Alfie. Their little family just makes my heart sing!

Thank you so much for your support. I am humbled by all the love readers continue to show me, my characters and our stories. I know that none of this would be possible without you.

Until the next time, please take care and may God's blessings be with you always.

With much love,

*Deborah Fletcher Mello*

www.DeborahMello.org

# COLTON 911: AGENT BY HER SIDE

---

## Deborah Fletcher Mello

HARLEQUIN
ROMANTIC
SUSPENSE

Special thanks and acknowledgment are given to
Deborah Fletcher Mello for her contribution to
the Colton 911: Grand Rapids miniseries.

**HARLEQUIN®**
ROMANTIC
SUSPENSE™

Recycling programs
for this product may
not exist in your area.

ISBN-13: 978-1-335-62672-1

Colton 911: Agent By Her Side

Copyright © 2020 by Harlequin Books S.A.

This edition published by arrangement with Harlequin Books S.A.

For questions and comments about the quality of this book,
please contact us at CustomerService@Harlequin.com.

Harlequin Enterprises ULC
22 Adelaide St. West, 40th Floor
Toronto, Ontario M5H 4E3, Canada
www.Harlequin.com

Printed in U.S.A.

A true Renaissance woman, **Deborah Fletcher Mello** finds joy in crafting unique story lines and memorable characters. She's received accolades from several publications, including *Publishers Weekly*, *Library Journal* and *RT Book Reviews*. Born and raised in Connecticut, Deborah now considers home to be wherever the moment moves her.

## Books by Deborah Fletcher Mello

### Harlequin Romantic Suspense

#### *Colton 911: Grand Rapids*

*Colton 911: Agent By Her Side*

#### *To Serve and Seduce*

*Seduced by the Badge*
*Tempted by the Badge*
*Reunited by the Badge*

### Harlequin Kimani Romance

*Truly Yours*
*Hearts Afire*
*Twelve Days of Pleasure*
*My Stallion Heart*
*Stallion Magic*
*Tuscan Heat*
*A Stallion's Touch*
*A Pleasing Temptation*
*Sweet Stallion*
*To Tempt a Stallion*
*A Stallion Dream*

Visit the Author Profile page at
Harlequin.com for more titles.

To my agent, Pattie Steele-Perkins

You continue to push me to step outside my comfort zone.

Your encouragement has been the wind beneath my wings.

I soar because you make me believe I can. Thank you!

# Chapter 1

"Happy birthday, Special Agent Winston!"

FBI Special Agent Cooper Winston looked up from the files on his desk. "Thank you, Agent Miller," he said, tossing a smile at the regal black woman who stood in the doorway of his office. "I thought I'd done a good job of keeping that a secret."

She chuckled softly. "I think you're good. I just remembered that you and my youngest daughter share the same birthday. She turned thirty-four today, but don't tell her I told you that!"

Cooper gestured for her to enter, pointing her to an upholstered chair in front of his desk. He and Claire Miller had worked together since he'd been transferred from the FBI's main office in Detroit to Grand Rapids on Ionia Avenue. She had backed him up on his first case and they'd been good friends ever since. He couldn't imagine the resident agency without her bright personality keeping them all on their toes.

Cooper laughed. "Your secret is safe with me!"

"So, how old are you now?" the older woman questioned, eyeing him with a raised brow.

Cooper smiled a second time. "This year makes forty."

"A milestone birthday! We should be celebrating that with cake and champagne in the break room."

He shook his head and waved a hand. "That's what we're not going to do," he said. "You and I are going to keep this between us and remain good friends as we do."

A bright smile filled her dark face. "I understand completely. I'll be a year closer to retirement and my pension on my next birthday."

"How long have you been with the agency?"

"Twenty-six years next month."

"Wow! Now you've definitely earned that pension but you don't look anywhere close to qualifying for retirement. We might need to check your birth certificate," he said teasingly.

"Aren't you sweet! They say a woman shouldn't share her age, but when you consider the alternative, I'm proud to tell people I'm fifty-four, almost fifty-five years young."

"I'd be proud, too, if I looked as good!"

Claire laughed warmly. "So, how is that beautiful baby boy of yours?"

Cooper's smile widened. He reached for the framed photo on his desk, passing it to the woman. "Alfie is doing very well. He keeps me on my toes!"

"Isn't he precious! Look how big he's gotten! I swear, they grow up too fast."

"No one warns you about that when they're born."

She laughed. "No, they surely don't." She passed the image back to him. "I hear you caught the RevitaYou case? How's that going?"

Cooper nodded, pointing to the stack of files he'd been reviewing when she knocked on his door. "I did. And it's not. I could have used your expertise tracking down my bad guy but they tell me you're hunting down that serial killer."

"Bagged him earlier this morning. We caught him in the act and now I have a boatload of paperwork to do and a trial to help the DA prepare for before I catch another assignment."

"Nice work, Agent!"

"Thank you. I appreciate that. Especially coming from you. I'll get out of your hair," Claire said. "I just wanted to say hello and acknowledge your day."

"I really appreciate that. Thank you."

"You're one of the good ones, Cooper. Keep doing what you do!"

As Claire made her exit, Cooper turned back to the paperwork that was proving to be problematic. Despite the information in each of the file folders, he was no closer to finding the now infamous Wes Matthews than he'd been when the case was first dropped in his lap.

Wes Matthews had been the brain trust behind RevitaYou, a supplement that promised to be the fountain of youth for users and a pot of gold for investors. The drug itself had been created by renowned chemist Landon Street. Initial forensic tests showed that RevitaYou was chock-full of vitamins and minerals, but also tested positive for ricin, an extremely deadly poison.

Ricin was found naturally in castor beans. It could also be made from the waste material left over from processing castor oil. Street had discovered that the initial oil compound he created did wonders for smoothing wrinkles, but somewhere along the way, the self-professed healer became "the Toxic Scientist," as the media dubbed him, doing harm to those he claimed to want to help. He had purposely poisoned people. Multiple deaths had been attributed to RevitaYou and both Street and Matthews were now in the wind. But not before Wes Matthews had disappeared with millions from unsuspecting backers in a pyramid investment scheme.

Now, finding both Matthews and Street was at the top of Cooper's to-do list.

He sighed, warm breath blowing past his lips. Frustration furrowed his thick brow. Since the start of this case he'd hit one dead end after another. Before Claire had walked into his office he'd been ready to fling the folders across the room. Now, he just needed to refocus, get back to work, and hope there were no more distractions.

"FBI tip line. How can we help you?" Kiely Colton said. She did her best to keep her expression staid, although her disposition that day was less than stellar.

"Is this the tip line?" a woman questioned.

Kiely tempered her tone. "Yes, ma'am. You've reached the FBI tip line. How can we help you?" she repeated.

"If what I tell you gets someone arrested, will I get a reward?"

"That all depends on what you report, ma'am."

"Good, 'cause I know some things!"

"Well, let's start with your name. Who am I speaking with?"

"My name?"

"Yes, ma'am. I'll need your name and address and a good contact number to reach you in case one of our agents needs to speak with you further."

"Let me call you back. I need to check some things," the woman said as she disconnected the line.

Kiely rolled her eyes skyward. Most of the calls she'd taken that morning had gone similarly. Concerned citizens were more interested in reward money than helping to catch criminals. One man even had the audacity to insist they pay him in advance for information he didn't yet have, about a robbery that had never been reported.

Claire laughed. "It's like that most days. I think it's something in the water."

"Or a full moon," Kiely said with a chuckle.

"We appreciate you coming in to help out. Most of our agents are out in the field. If this keeps up we're going to have to hire additional staff."

"It's not a problem," Kiely answered. "I might be a freelance PI most of the time, but my motives are purely selfish if I'm honest with you."

"You still trying to find your foster brother?"

Kiely nodded. "Yeah. The last time any of us spoke to him he was scared and on the run. Getting him home is the surest way to keep him safe."

"I understand. Let us know if there is anything we can do to help."

Kiely gave the woman a wave as she replaced her headset and adjusted it against her ears. She worked for the family business, Colton Investigations. Her services were often utilized by the local police, the FBI and sometimes the CIA, because she had a reputation for always getting results. Kiely wasn't above circumventing the rules to get the job done. Because she was trusted and required no handholding, she was routinely invited into the FBI's inner sanctum and given privileges few others were granted.

For the moment, Kiely volunteering to answer the phones was all about helping Brody Higgins. Brody was family to her and her five siblings, ever since their father, Graham Colton, had taken him under his wing. Before then, Brody had been lost in the foster system. He'd been a smart kid with a string of misdemeanors who found himself in the wrong place at the wrong time. When he caught a murder charge for a crime he didn't commit, their father, a prominent Michigan district attorney, had declined to prosecute, taking him into their home instead. Love and family had turned Brody's life around...or until recently.

Now Brody was tangled up in the RevitaYou scandal and running from people intent on doing him harm. Borrowing money from a loan shark to invest in RevitaYou then defaulting on that loan had made him a target. When Capital X, the predatory lending organization who'd fronted money to Brody had sent two goons to collect payment and he'd not been able to make good on his debt, they'd broken his fingers, promising to break more the next time they had to pay him a visit. Finding Wes Matthews, the charismatic criminal who'd drawn Brody into the whole mess, was a high priority for her. Kiely answered another call, and then a third and fourth. The tip line was suddenly flooded with incoming calls, pulling her attention from thoughts of Brody and Matthews.

Two hours, umpteen calls and only one credible tip later, and Kiely was ready to hang up her headset. Taking a quick glance down to the Apple Watch on her wrist, she realized it wasn't yet twelve noon. She needed to take a break and just as she pushed her chair from the desk, one last call rang for her attention. She sighed, pushing the button to answer the line.

"FBI tip line. How can we help you?"

A man's voice, deep and slightly muffled, sounded in her ear. "I have information about Wes Matthews, the Capital X and RevitaYou banker. I know where he is."

"Can you tell me your name, sir?" Kiely asked. She took a deep breath and held it. Goose bumps had risen on her arm after hearing Wes Matthews's name.

"No," the man said, his tone curt and short. "You just need to know that he's hiding out at Reeds Lake, off Lakeside Drive. There's a small, white cottage off the dirt road. He's there, but I don't know for how long."

"Sir, do you…" Kiely started, but a dial tone sounded in her ear, the caller disconnecting the call.

Kiely typed the information she'd received into the call screen, then jumped from her seat. Something about that tip registered on her radar and suddenly had her on edge. This was the one lead she planned to personally vet.

After conferring with one of the technicians she flung herself down the short length of corridor to the corner office with the door closed. Despite wanting to just take off, there were protocols Kiely still had to follow if she wanted to maintain a relationship with the FBI, and updating the agent handling the case was one of them. Unfortunately, the agent she needed to update was Cooper Winston, a man who riled her nerves more than most. He was way too straitlaced and slightly anal. She imagined he probably gave himself a headache due to always being so inflexible.

She knocked on the door but didn't wait to be welcomed inside. Kiely draped her frustration around her like a bold blanket. She couldn't begin to understand how such a handsome man could be so infuriating. And he was definitely handsome! His features were chiseled, looking like he'd been carved out of alabaster stone. With eyes that were oceanic blue and thick, reddish-blond hair combed back to tame the natural curl, he looked like a Celtic god. Or what Kiely imagined a Celtic deity should look like. Despite his good looks, he always seemed to take great joy in pushing her buttons and now his too-calm demeanor had her wanting to pull her hair out.

She moved further into his office and dropped down into the chair opposite him. She bit back the expletive on the tip of her tongue, instead focusing on the look he was giving her. There was something in his eyes that suddenly felt like a serious punch to her gut. Her stomach did a slight flip and she found it disconcerting, unable to explain it if she had to. She took a deep breath and held it, then blew it slowly past her lips, watching as he crossed his arms over his chest and leaned back against the metal desk.

As his door flew open and Kiely Colton entered, Cooper looked up, his eyes widening in surprise at the sight of her. Although he had heard she was in the office volunteering her services, he hadn't expected to see her. The two had history and little of it had been positive. They'd butted heads often when Kiely circumvented the rules to work a case her own way. He worked by the books, moving from *A* to *Z* without skipping *E*, *F* and *G*. Kiely Colton acted like she didn't know how to count from one to one hundred, her mathematical manipulations all over the place to get the right answers. He found her tendency to leap before looking infuriating. She was reckless, was rarely a team player, or nice, and he knew that behavior could put others in harm's way.

"What's going on?" he said, resting his ink pen against the yellow-lined notepad he'd been writing on.

"We've got a lead on Wes Matthews. I'm going to go check it out."

Cooper stood. "No, you're not."

"Excuse me?"

As Kiely's incredulous expression exploded, Cooper noted confusion, frustration and a hint of hostility detonating in real time. He lifted a brow as she continued.

"Are you kidding me, right now? I need to…"

He cut her off, stalling the rant he felt coming. "Calm down, Ms. Colton, and tell me what you know."

"We're wasting time," she snapped.

"And you're still a civilian," he quipped. "So, please, take a breath, and update me! So, what do you have?" he asked, his tone even and inquisitive.

"We just got a tip that Wes Matthews is hiding out in a cabin on Reeds Lake. I asked one of your agents to get me a satellite image and I want to go check it out. This might be the break we've been looking for."

"I'm inclined to think your tip is a hoax. We've gotten credible information that says Matthews is in the Caribbean, well out of our jurisdiction. He'd be a fool to still be here in Grand Rapids."

"Then he's a fool. My gut is telling me that the caller might be credible and it's well worth checking out."

He shook his head. "I think it's a waste of time and resources."

"You do know that I don't need your permission to follow up on a lead, right? That this is just a courtesy? Obviously, if I lay eyes on him, I'll immediately call for backup." Kiely's tone was defiant and determined. She moved onto her feet. "Because I am going!"

No woman should be so lovely and so darn exasperating, Cooper thought as he stood watching her. He hated to admit it, but he had honestly tried to forget how attractive she was. But having her in his space had made that harder for him to do. She wore black denim. The matching pants and jacket were flattering to her petite frame. The white blouse beneath it was crisply ironed and an FBI visitor's badge hung from a lanyard around her neck. Her makeup was sparse, just a hint of eyeliner and clear lip gloss complementing her crystal-clear complexion. Bangs and a shoulder-length bob highlighted her lush brown hair.

Cooper found the pout on her face unnerving, stirring heat in places that he was finding difficult to ignore. He shook the sensation away, shifting his focus to the door behind her. Despite his conjecture, she was determined to do what she wanted, whether he agreed or not. And he didn't agree, believing she was headed out on another wild-goose chase.

"Fine," he snapped as she moved toward the exit. "But I'm going with you."

"Excuse you?" Kiely stopped short, turning around to give him a look. "I don't need a babysitter."

"That's not why I'm going. The FBI received a tip and an FBI agent will follow up on that tip. Chain of command and all that," he said, moving his hand in a dismissive gesture.

"That's a stretch, don't you think?"

"I think that you interfering could be considered dangerous. What if something happens? Like you see him and he gets away because you didn't have backup? I'd hate to charge you with obstructing my investigation. So, you will not go without me going with you. Give me ten minutes and we can head that way."

Kiely shook her head, her frustration knee-deep. "Fine," she finally snapped. "But I'll drive."

By the time she was outside the office, standing at the bank of elevators, Kiely was not happy about the turn of events. She was very much a lone wolf when it came to the cases she investigated. Cooper's insistence that he join her was not sitting well and she felt like there would inevitably be a conflict with what she would need to do and what he would want her to do.

She watched him as he maneuvered around the office, moving from cubicle to cubicle. He dropped files onto desks and delegated orders. He had changed out of his black suit and was wearing khaki slacks and a dark blue nylon jacket with the prominent yellow FBI logo. She had always thought him attractive, but she hadn't realized just how gorgeous he really was. Because he *was* gorgeous. He was a tall powerhouse of defined muscle. His chiseled features and ginger-red hair made him model-pretty. His beard and mustache had been meticulously trimmed and his eyes were the most mesmerizing ocean blue.

As Kiely stared at him intently, his cell phone rang. He paused in the middle of the aisle and answered the call. The conversation was brief and clearly concerning. Kiely felt herself tense as the color drained from his face. He suddenly rushed toward where she stood, pushing past her as he hurried to the exit.

"What's wrong?" Kiely questioned, hurrying after him.

Cooper shot her a quick look. Resounding fear echoed in his voice as he answered, "My son Alfie is missing!"

## *Chapter 2*

They were a few good minutes away from the pre-school Cooper's young son attended. So, focused on getting there, Cooper seemed oblivious when Kiely slid into the passenger seat of his car. She said little to him, not even when he blew through three stop signs and barely stopped at the red light at the corner of Ionia and Fulton Streets. His frustration was palpable and growing exponentially. Kiely could only begin to imagine what he had to be feeling.

"Tell me about your son," she said softly, wanting to help center his focus.

Cooper told her he had chosen the Goodman Children's Center by default. Alfie had only been a few months old when he'd found the name of the day care and preschool in his late wife's papers. She had made a list of preschools shortly after discovering she was pregnant with their first child. The Goodman name had been circled in red at the very top of the page. "That was just like Sara, to make plans for our son before he was even born," Cooper shared with Kiely.

Sara had been his first love. They'd been the best of friends in college, both having an affinity for old movies and buttered popcorn tossed with M&M's candies. When their relationship became romantic it had surprised them both. One day they'd been bitterly debating the writings of William Faulkner and the next he was reading her John Keats as they fed each other strawberries slathered with whipped cream. Marriage had been a mere technicality, defining their relationship more so for others than themselves. From the moment they had claimed each other's hearts, nothing and no one could have kept them apart.

Sara had wanted children from the moment they said their vows. But getting pregnant hadn't been easy. There had been three miscarriages and both had given up hope, declaring themselves enough for each other. For a moment they had considered adoption but just days after completing the application, they discovered Sara was pregnant once again.

The pregnancy was immediately labeled high

risk and his beautiful wife had been confined to their bed for the duration. By the start of her third trimester she'd made lists for everything. Lists for schools. Lists for doctors. Lists for everything she hoped for their baby.

Surprisingly, labor and delivery had been a breeze. Alfred Cooper Winston arrived in the wee hours of August first, bellowing at the top of his tiny lungs. Cooper's last memory of them together as a family, joyous and happy, was when they laid the newborn on his wife's chest and she introduced herself, and him, to their newborn son. Minutes later, little Alfie was snatched from his mother's arms and hurried off to the nursery as they rolled Sara to the operating room. The doctors were unable to stall the postpartum bleeding. Sara had died on the table, never able to hold her young son again.

Cooper struggled with the memory and to keep driving. He could see Kiely fighting back her own tears out of the corner of his eye. "It was a rough time for me," he said.

"I'm so sorry for your loss," Kiely answered.

Cooper shrugged his broad shoulders. "After that I had to take care of Alfie and he became my entire world." He choked back a sob and when Kiely reached out for his hand, gently squeezing the back of his fingers, it took every ounce of his fortitude to contain the tears that pressed against his lashes.

Her touch was consoling and warm and there was comfort in her touch that he had not expected.

Cooper turned in the entrance gates, speeding past the playground of sandboxes and swing sets. When he reached the administration building and the parking lot, he pulled into the fire lane and shut down his vehicle. A team of local police cars lined the driveway, uniformed officers milling around the grass and steps outside the entrance.

Kiely followed on his heels as he hurried into the building, flashing his federal badge at the officer who stood to block his way. "It's my son who's missing!" he snapped.

"The parents are here," Kiely heard someone say into a radio, the person on the other end responding with an admonishment to let them enter. She tossed Cooper a look but he seemed to not have heard the comment, blinded by the emotion that had him in a vise grip.

The school's administrator met them at the door to the office. "Mr. Winston, I am so sorry," she said. "We're doing everything we can to…"

"What happened? Where's my son?" Cooper snapped harshly.

The other woman repeated herself. "I'm so, so sorry! He was outside for recess and someone just grabbed him."

"How did this person get on campus? And who

was supposed to be watching my son?" Cooper's voice rose two octaves, his emotion explosive. "I need answers. I want to know who saw what happened!"

A plainclothes detective rushed to Cooper's side. He held out his hand. "Agent Winston, my name is Detective Cranston. Will you come with me, please? We're reviewing the security tapes, and I need to know if you recognize anyone."

Kiely followed, standing at Cooper's elbow as they moved into the administrator's office. A team of police officers were all standing before a small video screen. Cooper pushed forward for a front row view.

There was no audio and the footage was grainy, but there was no missing the man standing outside by the gate that led into the toddler play area. He was dressed in a security guard's uniform and appeared to be on the job, wearing a ball cap, the brim pulled down low over his eyes. You couldn't see his face, but he was sizeable, with a beer gut and thick arms.

As the teacher and her assistant shuffled a group of eight kids from the play area back into the building, the man rushed forward and grabbed little Alfie. A dark sedan pulled up beside the two and just like that the child and the man were gone, the teacher screaming as she ran down the driveway after them.

"I tried to stop them," the young woman sobbed from across the room, where she sat talking to an officer. "I tried!"

"Does he look familiar to you, Agent?" Detective Cranston questioned, pausing the video on the image of the kidnapper.

Cooper shook his head. "No, I don't recognize him. But the uniform's off. The color is wrong. It's more army green. You can buy them at any military supply store. The security officers here wear a more military blue." Cooper sighed. "Do we know anything else?"

"No, sir," the detective said, "but we've issued an Amber Alert and all of my men are doing what we can to find your son. Right now, though, we need to ask you some questions." He gestured toward Kiely. "Another officer will speak with your wife."

Kiely shook her head. "I'm not his wife. I'm a private investigator."

The man narrowed his gaze and shot her a suspicious glance. "A private investigator?"

"Ms. Colton is partnered with the FBI on a case we're working," Cooper said, shifting his eyes back to the detective. "We were on another investigation when I got the call. Ms. Colton doesn't know my son."

The detective nodded. "Colton? We have a Sadie Colton working the case. She's an investigator. You're not related by chance, are you?"

Kiely said, "Sisters. Is Sadie here?"

He nodded. "Outside, I think."

Kiely pressed a warm palm against Cooper's forearm. "I'm going to go see what I can find out from my sister," she said, her voice dropping to a whisper meant only for his ears. "Are you going to be okay?"

"I'm not going to be okay until I get my son back," he muttered.

She locked gazes with Cooper. The look he gave her spoke volumes, the hurt in his heart monumental. He was clearly struggling to contain his emotion, wanting to rage and cry and still be strong for his son. Not wanting to be seen as weak to his colleagues. His concern for his child pulled at her heartstrings. Cooper the father wasn't nearly as hard and cold as Cooper the agent. His determination to find his son was impressive. She liked this Cooper a lot.

As they continued to stare into each other's eyes, it was a silent exchange that passed between them, words not needed. Kiely nodded her understanding. She squeezed his arm one last time.

"I'll be right back," she said softly.

Moving back to the parking lot, Kiely found her sister taking photos of tire tracks, the playground, and the landscape.

When Sadie looked up from what she was doing,

she was surprised to see her. "Hey there! What are you doing here?"

"Working."

Sadie looked confused.

"Long story short, Agent Winston and I were headed to check on a lead when he got the call about his son. I tagged along to see if there was anything I could do to help."

Sadie nodded. A former police rookie turned crime-scene investigator, Sadie approached all her cases pragmatically. "This was brazen. Broad daylight, other children and staff right there. Whoever snatched the kid wanted to be seen." She pointed at the multitude of cameras positioned to capture everything that moved. "There was nothing haphazard about this. They were sending his father a message. Any idea who might have a vendetta against him?"

Kiely shook her head. "He's a stickler for the law. It could be anyone he's ever crossed paths with. And I have no doubt, that list is miles long."

"What case were you investigating?"

"The FBI got a lead on Wes Matthews's whereabouts. We were headed to check it out."

"I'll keep my fingers crossed. The sooner we get Matthews, the sooner we can get Brody home."

"We haven't talked in a while. Everything good with you?" Kiely asked.

Sadie tossed a look over her shoulder, making

sure none of the other officers could hear her. "Tate wants to elope," she said casually.

The comment hit Kiely like a sledgehammer. Tate Greer was Sadie's fiancé. As far as Kiely was concerned, Tate was the product of bad sperm. He was egotistical and arrogant but deep down he was a coward who used others to make himself relevant. Everything about the man was a monumental red flag for the rest of the family. None of them were as charmed by him as their sister was. The two were like oil and water... snake oil and holy water, that is. But Tate had a viselike grip on her sister's heart. Kiely swallowed, slowly digesting the pronounce-ment. "Elope?"

Sadie nodded. "He wants us to sneak off to Las Vegas to get married."

"What happened to you two having a Christ-mas wedding?"

"Tate changed his mind."

"But you've always wanted a big wedding with bridesmaids and a ridiculous cake and a big white dress and all of us there with you. That's all you've ever talked about since we were all kids and you had a crush on Riley's friend Preston. Preston Richards with the Coke bottle glasses and that cowlick thing that always stuck up on his head. Remember?"

"I do, but Tate doesn't have any family and he thinks since we're going to be family that we should start our life together with it just being the two of us."

"You know how that sounds, right?"

"I think it's sweet! He's such a romantic and he just wants it to be a private celebration for the two of us and then we'll share it with everyone else afterward."

Nothing about it sounded romantic to Kiely. It sounded like Tate was trying to manipulate her sister. He tended to be overbearing and possessive. Because Sadie saw him with blinders on, Kiely found it best to say as little as possible about him when she could, not wanting to push her sister away and tighten the hold Tate had on her.

"What are you going to do?" Kiely questioned.

She made a mental note to call their other two sisters the first chance she got. An intervention was needed, she thought to herself. Sadie deserved so much better and Tate was not it. He professed to be in the import-export business but even that was questionable. Everything about Tate felt slimy, the man not having an ounce of substance equal to Sadie's intellect and compassion. But Sadie, who'd always been very much a late bloomer when it came to men and sex, apparently saw nothing but golden opportunities with the man.

"And don't tell anyone," Sadie said, seeming to read Kiely's mind. "I still don't know what I plan to do."

"As long as you don't plan to do anything before we have a chance to talk more," Kiely responded.

Movement by the school doors drew both their attention, cutting their conversation short. Cooper had stepped outside, pulling his cell phone to his ear as the door slammed closed behind him. He stepped away from the two officers standing guard. Something about his tense body language triggered Kiely's radar.

"I need to run," she said, tossing her sister a look. "I'll call you later."

"Is that the father?" Sadie asked, looking toward where Kiely was staring.

"Yeah."

Sadie hummed. "Interesting...very interesting."

Kiely cut her eye at her sibling. "Goodbye, Sadie!"

"Love you, too!"

The image on Cooper's cellphone screen read NO CALLER ID. Reception inside the school had been spotty and so he'd stepped outside. "Hello?"

"Is this Agent Winston?" Cooper didn't recognize the female voice on the other end and the private number she was calling him on wasn't one he gave out readily. His anxiety level suddenly increased tenfold and he felt the knot in his midsection tighten.

"Who is this?" Cooper asked.

"I have your son. If you want to see him again, drop the search for Wes Matthews," she said.

"Who is this?" Cooper said, his voice rising as his pulse hammered. He could feel his pulse thumping loudly in his head, his heart about to burst from his chest.

"Drop the search," she repeated, "if you want your kid back." Then she hung up, disconnecting the call.

Cooper leaned forward, his hands on his knees. He could barely breathe and his vision blurred. He felt like he might vomit and suddenly he wanted to hit something. He turned and kicked the wooden handrail. Hard. When he'd dislodged one of the balusters, he stopped. He inhaled deeply and then again. He couldn't believe this was happening. That someone would go after his family to get to him. Keeping his son safe was the single most important responsibility he had, and suddenly he felt like he had failed. He had let Alfie down and he imagined his baby boy had to be petrified, not understanding what was going on. Cooper struggled not to rage. He needed a moment to collect himself and his thoughts to figure out what his next steps should be.

He suddenly slapped the smartphone against his leg just as Kiely reached his side. "Who was that?" she asked, as he stood up to stare at her.

"I don't know but she said she had Alfie and that I need to stop searching for Wes Matthews if I want him back."

"She actually mentioned Matthews?"

He nodded.

* * *

Kiely's mind was suddenly racing. First the FBI got a tip about where Matthews might be hiding out, and now this. She didn't believe in coincidences, and as the two stood staring at each other she realized he didn't either. He suddenly started texting fiercely, almost pounding the keys on his phone with his thumbs.

"It's a long shot," he said, "but I'll see if our techs can track this. But I'm betting it was a burner. There was no caller ID and the call barely lasted sixty seconds."

"I'll understand if you need to stay here, but I'm going to follow up on that tip. If someone doesn't want us to find Wes Matthews, then we need to find him. That may also help us find your son."

Cooper nodded. "I was thinking the same thing. But if anything happens here, Detective Cranston can call me. You're not going alone and if there's any chance that this could lead me to my son I want to be there."

There was a moment of hesitation as Kiely stared at him. Cooper the agent and Cooper the father were holding hands, both intent on finding his son. She admired his determination, reminded of her own father who would have moved mountains to protect her and her siblings. Knowing there would be no talking him out of it, Kiely nodded her agreement as Cooper dialed a number on his phone.

"Who are you calling?" she questioned.

"Something tells me we might need some help," he said.

Kiely met the intense look he was giving her. Having decided to press forward, he had determination emitting from his eyes. She had high regard for his devotion to his son and his job. A lesser man would have been brought to his knees. It moved her and she had greater respect for him.

She nodded again. "Backup is good," she said.

# Chapter 3

An hour later Cooper had assembled an entire team. Grand Rapids Police Detective Emmanuel Iglesias and Lieutenant Tripp McKellar stood with them in the parking lot of a local Realtor's office located one mile from their target location: Matthews's alleged hideout on Reeds Lake. A ten-member SWAT team stood by, waiting for instructions.

"Kiely, have you met Lieutenant McKellar?" Emmanuel asked.

Kiely and Emmanuel had been acquainted for some time. Emmanuel was engaged to her twin sister. This was not their first time working together, and she appreciated having him by her side...but she'd never met Tripp.

"I don't believe I have," Kiely said. She extended her hand. "Kiely Colton. It's a pleasure."

"Kiely is Pippa's twin," said Emmanuel. "She's also a private investigator."

"The pleasure is all mine," Lieutenant McKellar responded. "Your reputation precedes you."

"Not sure if that's a good thing!" Kiely said with a nervous chuckle. She could only begin to imagine the stories her sister and Emmanuel might have told him about her, the two over exaggerating her antics.

Cooper looked from her to the other man. Kiely noticed his jaw tighten slightly, as if their small talk was beginning to annoy him. "Everyone ready?" he asked.

There was an exchange of looks, the trio nodding their heads.

"More than ready," Kiely said. "Are you sure you want to do this?" She asked the question, concerned that him worrying about his son, he might not be as focused as they needed him to be.

"I'll be fine," Cooper answered. And for the most part he was, he thought. They didn't know how credible the tip was or if it would lead them to Alfie, but doing something felt better than sitting around waiting for others to report back to him. He gave her a nod of his head.

"Then let's do this," she said.

The four drove to the end of the dirt road and parked the black SUV. The SWAT team members followed. Exiting the vehicle, their plan was to walk the short distance to the home and execute a knock and enter once they assessed the situation. There had been no time for a search warrant, and no one wanted to risk violating anyone's rights and blowing the case. The SWAT team members would hold their position until needed.

The area was wooded, tall pine trees decorating the landscape and affording them a measure of cover. As they made their way to the small white cottage with the shuttered windows, Cooper gestured for Emmanuel to take one side and Tripp to take the other. When he motioned for Kiely to fall in behind him, she thought to argue but didn't.

Movement by the window caught her eye. A woman shuffled past once and then a second time in the opposite direction. All the windows were open, a slight breeze blowing their sheer white curtains aside. The sound of a child crying echoed through the air.

"Enough," the woman said, her loud tone filtering out the kitchen window. "I said I'd get you a snack. You need to stop that damn crying."

Her brusque manner only made the child cry harder.

"It's Alfie," Cooper whispered.

He took a step and Kiely grabbed the back of his jacket. The look she gave him spoke volumes. She understood him wanting to rush in but they needed to proceed cautiously. They didn't want anyone to get hurt, most especially his little boy. Until they could assess who and how many persons were inside, they needed to stand down.

Cooper nodded his understanding, inhaling deeply to quell his anxiety. Moving swiftly, they approached the home prudently. Kiely took cover behind a tree as Cooper took the steps, his weapon drawn. Inside, the child suddenly cried out as if in pain. His little scream was gut-wrenching, even to Kiely. Evidently unable to contain himself a moment longer Cooper became less an agent and more a father as he rushed the door, Kiely covering his back.

Shots, fired from the inside and through the front entrance, sounded one after the other.

Bang!

Bang!

Bang!

All three shots splintered the wood door and hit Cooper square in the chest. The blow sent him backward down the stairs as Kiely screamed his name.

The moment was suddenly surreal. Shots were fired in the rear yard of the home. The child crying inside sounded hysterical. Kiely moved swiftly to the bottom of the steps to check on Cooper. Blood had begun to pool behind his head. She searched for a pulse and nodded at Lieutenant McKellar who knelt beside her. The lieutenant radioed for backup and an ambulance as Kiely continued up the steps and into the home.

Clearing the first two rooms, she rushed to the kitchen, arriving at the back door just as a woman dressed from head to toe in black jumped onto an older model Kawasaki motorcycle and took off through the line of pine trees. Emmanuel jumped into the back of a black SUV, the police in pursuit. Moving swiftly back into the house, Kiely found Alfie huddled in the bathtub, his little arms wrapped around his knees as he rocked back and forth. He was so tiny, she thought, and he looked fragile. Her heart burst, a wave of emotion flooding her spirit as she eyed him. She suddenly wanted to scoop him up into her arms and hug him like her mother use to hug her when she was afraid.

Kiely secured her weapon and held up her hands as if she were surrendering. She waved her fingers, doing jazz hands.

"Hi there," she said softly. "You must be Alfie."

His eyes widened at the mention of his name. But fear still emanated from his eyes.

Kiely knelt beside the tub, meeting the child at eye level. "Alfie, my name is Kiely. I'm a friend of your daddy. I'd like to be your friend, too."

The little boy's eyes were still locked on her.

He pulled his thumb into his mouth and continued to rock.

She looked around the room. "This place isn't very nice, is it?" She made a funny face, wiggling her nose. "Would you like to come with me, Alfie?" she said.

There was a moment of hesitation as the child seemed to be considering his options and then he reached both arms out, standing to wrap them around her neck. Kiely blew a warm sigh of relief as she lifted him up into her arms and hugged him tightly. "That's a good baby." By the time Kiely reached the front door and the steps, little Alfie had fallen asleep on her shoulder.

She moved to the ambulance just as they lifted Cooper inside. "Is he okay?" she questioned. His eyes were closed and his breathing seemed labored. Not knowing the extent of his injuries, she could feel her fear rising swiftly, her heart beginning to beat rapidly. She wasn't sure if he was asleep, unconscious, or perched on the edge of his deathbed.

The EMS responder nodded. "He took a hard hit to the back of his head when he fell. He might have a concussion and he's definitely going to need stitches. And today was his lucky day. His vest caught the bullets. But he's going to feel that tomorrow and will probably be sore for a few days."

Kiely blew a soft sigh. She was flooded with a wave of relief at the good news. She tightened her hold on the little boy who would wake up needing his daddy, grateful that would be able to happen.

Stepping up into the ambulance Kiely reached for his hand. She leaned down to whisper into his ear. "Alfie's here, Cooper," she said. "We found him and he's safe."

His eyes fluttered open, closed, then opened a second time. He struggled to focus as he squeezed her fingers tightly. The faintest smile pulled at his lips. He reached a shaky hand out to touch his son, pressing his fingers to Alfie's back. Relief visibly flooded his body.

Cooper sputtered as he struggled to get his words out. "Don't…don't leave…don't leave him, Kiely. Please…don't leave him."

"He's safe," she answered. "I'm going with you both to the hospital so he can be checked out, but he's fine."

Cooper shook his head. His eyes were wide, a hint of desperation shimmering in the oceanic orbs. His grip on her fingers was almost crushing. "Promise…please! Don't let my son out of your sight," he implored.

Kiely nodded her head. "I promise," she said softly as she tightened her grip on the little boy. "I won't take my eyes off him."

Alfie slept so soundly that Kiely wasn't sure if she should be nervous or not. He really was a cute little thing, she thought as she sat by the hospital crib staring down at him. He had a head of wavy blond hair, the chubbiest cheeks flushed a warm shade of pink, and his father's blue eyes. He smiled in his sleep, seeming to dream peacefully.

Dr. Mara Finley, the resident pediatrician at Butterworth Hospital, had decided to keep him overnight for observation, wanting to ensure that all was well with Alfie after his traumatic experience. He'd had a warm sponge bath, eaten grapes and spaghetti for supper, then had lay back in Kiely's lap as he watched an episode of some cartoon called *Peppa Pig* until he drifted back to sleep.

As promised, Kiely had not left his side since he'd been admitted. A nurse had been kind enough to give her an update on his father. Cooper had two cracked ribs, twelve stitches to close the gash in the back of his head and a confirmed concussion. According to her sources, he, too, was sleeping soundly.

Standing, she pulled a pale yellow blanket up over Alfie's shoulders. He'd kicked his covers off and the room had a chill. Continuing to watch him, his bottom lip quivering slightly, Kiely found herself awed by the turn of events. Of the women in her family, her sisters often joked that Kiely wouldn't know a maternal instinct if it stood up and slapped her. Growing up she had not been interested in playing with dolls and as an adult wasn't particularly fond of most children. In her mind, babies were like mini aliens and any place children gathered en masse was free birth control. It usually took less than an hour of them screaming and crying for her to dismiss the idea of kids in her life. Babysitting anyone's offspring had never been on her bucket list of things to do…before now.

She sat back in the pushback recliner, engaging the footrest as she lifted her legs and settled down for the night. She'd stay, she thought, only because she'd given Cooper her word. Tomorrow she'd have to rethink her plans to find Wes Matthews.

"Hi!"
"Hi!"
"Hi!"

The tiniest voice pierced her dreams and when Kiely opened one eye to see where it was coming from Alfie Winston was standing at the rail of the crib staring down at her.

When he saw that she was awake, the brightest smile pulled full and wide across his little face. "Hi!" he chirped again.

Kiely smiled and sat upright. "Good morning! How are you?" She stretched her arms out and then stood up, moving to the side of the crib. "You're looking good, kiddo!" She brushed a lock of curls from his eyes.

He bounced up and down. "Pan-pakes, peas?"

Kiely paused for a split second trying to ascertain what he was asking her. "Pancakes? You want pancakes?"

Alfie bounced again. "Peas! Pan-pakes!" he exclaimed, giggling excitedly.

"Pancakes are his favorite breakfast food." Cooper's voice suddenly came from the direction of the doorway. Kiely turned to look and saw a nurse pushing him in a wheelchair. "And he remembered to say please! I'm impressed."

Kiely turned toward him. "Good morning!"

"Dad-dy!" Alfie gushed, jumping up and down excitedly. "Dad-dy! Dad-dy!"

Cooper stood, moving to his son's side and lifting him into his arms. He kissed the child's cheek and hugged him to his broad chest. Alfie was still bobbing up and down, his infectious enthusiasm making them all laugh.

"Careful, Mr. Winston!" the nurse admonished. "You're not supposed to be lifting anything."

"Calm down, son. Daddy hurts!" Cooper said. He winced, as if pain was shooting through his torso.

"Maybe you should sit down," Kiely said, concern washing through her.

"That would probably be a good idea," the nurse said.

Cooper fell back into the seat Kiely had just va-

cated, settling Alfie against his lap. His son hugged him tightly.

"Looks like he missed you as much as you missed him," Kiely said, giggling softly.

"I definitely missed him," Cooper said, smiling. He kissed the child's cheek one more time.

"Dad-dy! Pan-pakes, peas?" Alfie repeated.

"I'll go to the nurses' station and call down to the cafeteria to see if we can do something about those pancakes," the nurse said. "Meanwhile, sir, please be careful."

"Thank you," Kiely said.

As the nurse exited the room, closing the door after herself, Kiely turned her attention back to Cooper. He was nuzzling his face into Alfie's hair, both of them calm and joyed to be back together. There was no denying the bond between them. Cooper the single father was clearly in love with the little boy now sitting in his lap, the wealth of his commitment to the child wholeheartedly evident. It felt slightly intrusive to be watching them so keenly but Kiely was touched by the sight of them together, their relationship pulling at her heartstrings.

She excused herself from the room, moving into the bathroom to give them a quiet moment together. She also had to pee, her bladder feeling like it might explode. Relief came quickly and as she stood washing her hands and staring at her reflection in the mirror, she found herself curious about Cooper the man, wanting to know more about him. There was clearly a side to him that she didn't know well. A side that was far less stringent and definitely more relaxed. That man seemed extremely interesting!

She pulled a hand through the length of her hair and pinched her cheeks for a hint of color to warm her face. Not that she was vain, but it didn't hurt to not look like she'd been through a torrential storm, she thought, especially since she needed a shower and wasn't feeling quite so fresh.

As she moved back into the room, Alfie gave her another bright smile and Kiely smiled back. When he suddenly reached out his arms toward her, she was surprised.

"Down!" the little boy said.

Jumping from Cooper's lap, Alfie ran to her, wrapping himself around her legs in a quick hug. He reached his arms up again, imploring her to lift him.

"What's up, buddy?" Kiely said as she reached down to pick him up.

Alfie leaned his head against her shoulder and began to play with the gold chain around her neck.

"He really likes you," Cooper said. There was no missing the slight surprise in his tone.

Kiely laughed. "As opposed to his father not liking me?"

"Who said I didn't like you?"

Kiely shrugged her shoulders. "We haven't always seen eye to eye."

"If I didn't like you, I would never have asked you to take responsibility for my son."

The look he gave her was suddenly unsettling, so Kiely changed the subject. "So, did the doctors say when you can go home?" she asked.

"Not yet, but I'm hoping we'll be out of here by this afternoon."

Before Kiely could respond, her cell phone vibrated in her pocket. She gestured for Cooper to give her a minute, shifting Alfie against her hip as she answered the call. Holding the child was so natural that it barely registered on her radar that she was maneuvering him and her phone at the same time. It was as easy as walking and chewing gum.

"Hello?"

Cooper swallowed hard, his stomach doing a slight flip as he watched Kiely standing there with his son in her arms. The boy was clearly comfortable with her and he had never before seen Alfie respond to any woman so affectionately. Not that he had introduced many women into his son's life. He had not made time or effort for any relationship since Sara's death. Cooper truly didn't believe that he would ever again love another woman as much as he had loved his late wife. He had convinced himself that it would only be him and Alfie together until Alfie left to go find his way in the world.

The conversation was quick and when he heard

Kiely express her gratitude to Lieutenant McKellar, he shook himself from the reverie he'd fallen into, shifting his gaze back to her face.

"Thank you," Kiely was saying. "We appreciate that." As she disconnected the call Alfie pulled her cell phone from her hands, then kicked his legs to be put down.

Kiely laughed. "Where are you going with my phone, buddy?"

Cooper shook his head. "He loves a telephone. Doesn't have a clue how to use one, but he loves to play with it."

"He's really a good baby," she said. "Not that I have a lot of experience with them. But he's quiet and he doesn't cry a lot."

"Trust me." Cooper laughed. "He has his moments."

Kiely shifted the conversation a second time. "That was McKellar on the phone. He's on his way here to update us. I told him we'd be here in Alfie's room. I hope that's okay?"

"That's fine. Let's hope he has some good news for us."

An awkward silence descended upon the room as they both sat watching Alfie. He was pushing buttons on Kiely's smartphone, enamored each time the screen changed. As they watched Alfie, he realized they were also watching each other, stealing glances when they thought the other wasn't looking.

Pancakes arrived minutes later and Kiely helped feed the little boy as Cooper sat and watched. The child's excitement over his pancake and syrup made her laugh. He ate with gusto, then polished off a handful of grapes and drank a container of milk.

"Does he always eat like this?" Kiely questioned.

Cooper laughed heartily. "He inherited my appetite."

The knock on the door pulled them both from the moment.

"Come in," Cooper said.

Tripp poked his head into the room, looking from one to the other. "Good morning! I hope I'm not interrupting?"

"Not at all. Come on in." Cooper gestured for the man to enter. He reached out his arm to shake Tripp's hand.

"You definitely look better than you did yesterday. How are you feeling?" Tripp asked.

Cooper nodded. "Like I was hit by a bus."

"Three direct hits from a .45, I imagine you would. Thank God you were wearing your vest!"

"We get any leads?"

"Nothing. My guys lost the driver almost immediately. That road she took through the woods became too narrow for the chase car about five miles in. We're searching traffic cameras now to see if we can figure out where she came out and where she went from there."

"What about the house?" Cooper asked.

"We swept the entire cabin and came up empty. A few partial fingerprints that came back with nothing. But what I can tell you is that Wes Matthews is the legal owner of the property. He purchased the house last year through one of the shell companies that the FBI had tied back to him previously. The neighbors say no one has ever lived there."

Kiely summarized the timeline that they did know. "So, we get an anonymous tip telling us where we might find Matthews hiding out. As that call is coming in someone snatches Alfie, then they contact you to insist you stop looking for Matthews. We discover Alfie and one of his kidnappers at the location we were told we'd find Matthews. And Matthews is still out there in the wind somewhere."

Kiely and Cooper exchanged a look, their gazes lingering for a brief moment.

"We still have more questions than answers," Cooper finally said.

"My men are still on it and I'll update you as soon as we get something," Tripp added.

"Thank you."

"Under the circumstances, we're going to keep you under surveillance for a few days. Until we can figure out who took your son, we can't be certain you're safe. We've posted an officer outside your door and there'll be a car in front of your home."

"I appreciate that," Cooper said with a nod, "but it really isn't necessary. I'm sure we'll be fine."

"The city of Grand Rapids insists," Tripp concluded.

For a moment Cooper thought to argue and then he looked at Alfie who had eased next to Kiely, holding onto her arm with a tight grip. His eyes were wide, something like fear shimmering in the blue orbs. His son was vulnerable and his kidnapping yesterday proved Cooper couldn't always protect him. There were going to be times he needed help. This might very well be one of those times, he thought as he pondered the ramifications of every bad thing that could possibly happen. He took a deep breath before responding. "Thank you," he said finally.

Tripp gave him an understanding nod. "Let me know if we can do anything else to help."

"Just stay on the case," Cooper concluded. "I really want to get this guy!"

Tripp shook his hand one last time. He winked an eye at Kiely who gave him a wave and then he made his exit.

Cooper looked from her to the door and back. Was Tripp flirting with her, he wondered. Was she enjoying the attention from the other man? And why was it suddenly bothering him? He shook the thoughts away, turning back as Kiely wiped syrup from Alfie's face and hands.

Another knock on the door turned all three heads. Doctors Mara Finley and Joshua Camp entered together.

"They told me I'd find you here," Dr. Camp said. He extended his hand to shake Cooper's, then introduced himself to Kiely. He was a small man with a very large mustache and a bald head. He had a booming voice that seemed to fill the room. "This must be Alfie!" he said as he leaned down to the little boy's level and gave him a high five.

"I should probably step out," Kiely said, her voice dropping as she gave Cooper a look.

He shook his head. "No, it's fine. I'd like you to stay. Please."

Dr. Finley had moved to Alfie's side. She ran a hand across his brow. "I think Alfie's ready to go home. All his tests came back fine. He slept well through the night and from this empty plate, I see he's eating well."

"He's definitely eating well." Kiely chuckled.

"How's Dad feeling?" Dr. Camp questioned. He was pressing a stethoscope to Cooper's back and chest, listening to his breath sounds.

"Ready to go home, too!"

"And we can make that happen but I need you to understand that home is where you're going to need to stay. It's going to be at least six weeks before you can go back to work."

"Six weeks!" Cooper's eyes widened, his mind

beginning to race as he considered how he could make that work. He still had a case to solve and his son to care for. Recuperating would come with some challenges he wasn't quite prepared for.

The doctor nodded. "A minimum of six weeks and that's if you do everything I tell you to do to the letter. Do you have family close who can help?"

Cooper shook his head. "It's just me and Alfie. My dad lives in Boca Raton with his sister. If I need him to come he will, but I'll be able to work it out."

The doctor looked toward Kiely for a split second as he continued to talk. "Your treatment is going to be a combination of rest, pain management and breathing exercises. Rest being crucial which is why I asked about help. Not only will it reduce the pain, but it'll allow your body to navigate the healing process. You should get up and walk around but don't push yourself. No lifting anything over ten pounds. No contact sports. No high-impact activities. And no golf."

"No golf!"

"Your swinging will cause you excruciating pain."

"Do you play golf?" Kiely questioned.

Cooper shook his head and laughed. "No."

She smiled. "So, what can he do?"

"Starting next week, and let me repeat that, next week, you can return to low-impact activities. Light housework, and simple errands, but nothing that involves any heavy lifting or physical exertion. So that means you can sit at your desk but you definitely can't go out in the field."

"Anything else, Doctor?" Cooper asked.

"You can also resume sexual activity. Just remember to take it easy. No swinging from the chandeliers or anything too strenuous."

"That shouldn't be a problem," Cooper muttered.

Cooper saw Kiely blush, and knew his face was as red as hers. Neither doctor seemed to notice as he focused his attention on Alfie.

"Then, sir, I think we should be able to release you this afternoon. Someone from respiratory therapy will be up to show you some breathing exercises. Deep breathing is important but it's going to be painful for a while. We don't want to risk you getting pneumonia or any other respiratory illness right now."

"Thank you, Doctor," Cooper said.

Dr. Finley gave Kiely a light pat on the back. "Make sure he continues to eat well. And in two weeks schedule an appointment with his pediatrician just to follow up. But I don't think you're going to have any problems with this little guy. He's healthy and he's happy."

When both physicians were gone Cooper turned his attention to Kiely. "I'd like to enlist your services."

"Excuse me?"

"If anything happens, there's not much I'm going

to be able to do. I need security for Alfie. And I'm going to need someone to help me with him. He likes you so it just makes sense."

"So, you want to hire me?"

"Or you could volunteer your services."

Kiely repeated herself. "So, you want to hire me?"

Cooper laughed. "If you're available? And we can continue to work on the case together remotely from my home. It would be a win-win situation for both of us."

Alfie suddenly squealed, something on the television evidently tickling his funny bone. His laugh was infectious, feeling like a thick explosion of happy billowing through the room. Without giving it a second thought, Kiely nodded her head. "Yes," she said. "I can do that!"

# Chapter 4

"I am so confused!" Pippa Colton exclaimed. "So, now you're going to be a nanny?"

Kiely rolled her eyes skyward, throwing a pile of sweaters into the oversized suitcase she was packing. Once Alfie had fallen asleep for a nap, Cooper curled up in the hospital bed beside him, she'd come home to take a quick shower and pack a week's worth of clothes. She had a good hour before she had to be back at the hospital to pick up the two to take them home. She had more than enough time to go through her mail, set the DVR to record her favorite reality show, and drop her cat off at her sister's house. The long-haired Birman named Jim

Morrison brushed against her leg as if he knew he was going on a trip and he was ready to leave.

"Keep up, Pip! I'm working with the FBI agent handling the RevitaYou case. He was injured, his son was kidnapped and rescued and now he needs someone to help him out to keep the kid safe."

"You hate kids, Kiely. How is that going to work?"

"I don't hate kids. I just don't like them much. But this one's sweet."

"I don't know about that. I don't know if I'd trust you with any kid of mine."

"Thanks for the vote of confidence!"

Pippa laughed. "Seriously! I don't think I've ever seen you with anyone's kid. I don't know if you'd be any good at it. Is this one walking and talking so he can at least scream for help in case you do something wrong?"

"I don't know why I called you."

"I'm sure you just wanted my sage advice. So how long is this gig?"

"Just a few weeks. I'm going to be staying at his house while he recovers."

"His house? What about his wife?"

"He doesn't have a wife. Little Alfie's mother died in childbirth."

"Oh, my goodness! That's so sad!"

"It really is," Kiely said dropping down against the side of her bed. She reached for her cell phone and took it off speaker, pulling the device to her ear. "I almost cried when he told me what happened."

"So, he's single?"

Kiely didn't bother to answer her twin. Instead, she changed the subject. "I saw Emmanuel yesterday. We worked a raid together."

"He told me. He said you almost got yourself killed."

"I didn't get shot. The FBI agent did."

"That's so not cool. That could've been you. This entire case is wreaking havoc on my nerves."

"Speaking of, have you heard anything more from Brody?" Kiely knew that if anyone would hear from their foster brother it would be Pippa. The two were close and Brody trusted her more than anyone else.

"No, and it's driving me crazy. I'm worried to death that he might be out there hurt, with no one to help him."

"He'll be okay," Kiely said, her tone consoling.

Pippa blew a heavy sigh. "I hope you're right."

Kiely changed the subject again, hoping to shift the mood. "How are your wedding plans coming along? Have you and Emmanuel set a date?"

"They're coming. I think I want all my bridesmaids to wear pink."

"I'm not wearing pink, Pippa! Oh, hell no!"

"You'll wear pink for me."

Kiely groaned. "Only because we shared a womb. I wouldn't do it for anyone else."

Kiely hadn't been sure what to expect, but she was surprised by the sizable twenty-four-hundred square foot home in East Grand Rapids. The location was one of the most desired in the East Grand Rapids school system and proximity to downtown Gaslight Village. She imagined that it must have cost him a mint. He seemed to read her mind.

"We had two incomes when Sara and I purchased this house. It was her dream come true. We moved in just weeks before Alfie was born. I thought about moving after she died but I knew she wanted to raise our son here. The insurance money paid off the mortgage, so it only made sense to stay. I've been able to maintain it on my own since then."

Inside, the open floor design featured a large kitchen with a granite center island, slate appliances, a main floor master suite and bath, three additional extremely spacious bedrooms and an attached three-car garage. There was an expansive bonus room on the second floor and the home also had a full, finished basement with a private exit to the outside. The entire yard was fenced, there was a private back patio with a bricked-in grill and a meticulously landscaped lawn.

The decor was sparse and very masculine. The furniture was dark leather and except for the multitude of toys splayed around the rooms, there was little color. Alfie's room was the brightest spot in the home. The walls had been painted a lovely shade of mint green and white built-in bookcases and a desk decorated the space.

"Excuse the mess," Cooper said. "I wasn't expecting company, so I didn't clean up."

"It's fine," Kiely responded.

"I usually do make an effort to pick up the toys."

Kiely smiled. Alfie was toddling around the room, excited to be back in familiar space.

Cooper pointed to the Jack and Jill bathroom and the bedroom on the opposite side. "You're welcome to take the adjoining room there, or if you want, you can stay down in the basement. It's more private and has its own little kitchenette. The baby monitor is wired into the sound system through the whole house so you'd still be able to hear Alfie if he were up here and you were down there. You'd just have farther to walk."

"This will be fine," Kiely said as she moved through the bathroom and into the second bedroom. It was a very pretty space with a simple crocheted bedspread and matching pillows.

"I'll need to find the extra bedsheets and make up the bed," he said.

"You need to go lay down." Kiely shook her index finger at him. "The doctors told you to rest.

With your permission, I'm sure I'll be able to find everything I need."

"I am tired," Cooper said. "And please, feel free to help yourself to anything that will make this easy for you."

"Thank you. Now go take a nap. Alfie and I will be fine. He and I are going to make dinner."

"He can be a handful," Cooper said. "I just want to warn you."

Kiely laughed. "So can I!"

Cooper tossed and turned for almost thirty minutes. The pain pill he'd taken had relieved much of the hurt he'd been feeling but he couldn't turn his brain off long enough to relax and drift off to sleep. For the first fifteen minutes he'd listened to the baby monitor in the family room, eavesdropping on Kiely's conversation with his son.

She cooed and Alfie chattered back, the two seeming to have developed a language all their own. Then there'd been the rattle of pots and pans and the entire time Kiely talked to Alfie, even pausing now and again to ask him a question. There were many yes and no responses and an abundance of laughter that brought a smile to his face as he imagined the antics the duo were up to. After a few minutes he cut off his speaker and tried again to go to sleep, but he couldn't get Kiely off his mind.

As much as he knew about Kiely Colton, there

was probably twice as much that he didn't know. And he knew much about her father. Graham Colton had been one of Michigan's best state district attorneys. He was respected in the community, and his legal expertise, commitment to fairness in justice, and his dedication to service made him one of the good guys. He and his wife Kathleen had been pillars of the community. Her philanthropic interests and dedication to their children had made her a role model for many women. Sadly, the two were killed in an automobile accident, hit by a drunk driver as they returned home from the Michigan Governor's Service Award ceremony where Graham Colton had been honored just hours earlier. The loss to the family and the community had been devastating.

Their eldest son, Riley, had been with the agency during that time and Cooper remembered well how he had pulled his siblings together to get them through that tragedy and keep them standing. His eventual resignation to open Colton Investigations had been a loss for the FBI. Since then the Colton family had worked with the agency when help had been needed on other cases. Cases that had sometimes put him and Kiely at odds with one another. Now, here she was, in his home, caring for his son, and by default, him, too.

It probably would have been easier, Cooper thought, if she wasn't so darn beguiling. Kiely was a beauty and her carefree spirit gave him many reasons to pause. It had been some time since any woman had captured his attention. She had gotten under his skin, threatening to spread like wildfire and he wasn't sure how he felt about that. He struggled with what could have happened had she gone to check out that tip without him. If she had taken those bullets when things went left. The mere thought cut deep, reawakening feelings of loss he hadn't felt since his wife had died. Had anything happened to Kiely he would have been devastated.

He took a slow, deep breath, wincing as the sheer effort of doing so was painful. Closing his eyes, he thought briefly about going back to the family room to sit with his son and the woman who had his child equally captivated. He had questions he wanted to ask her. What was her favorite color? Her favorite food? Did she believe in monogamy? Was she dating anyone? Did she think he acted like a bumbling fool when he was in her presence?

He thought about her smile and the wisps of bangs that he always wanted to push out of her eyes. He thought about the way she sometimes stood with both hands in her back pockets, her tiny waist accentuating the fullness of her bustline. He imagined the feel of her in his arms. Wondered what she might taste like if he ever had opportunity to kiss her lips. Because he really wanted to kiss her lips and then just like that, Cooper felt himself drifting off into a deep sleep as Kiely walked through his dreams.

* * *

When Alfie was down for his own nap, Kiely stood in the doorway of Cooper's office. The wood-paneled space was reminiscent of an old English library with ceiling-high bookcases stretching across two walls. An oversized desk sat room center and a large globe decorated the corner. Stacks of manila folders covered the desktop, while Cooper's college degree, Quantico certification, numerous awards and accolades decorated one wall. The space was comfortable and she got the impression that Cooper spent far too much time in that one room.

There were a half-dozen pictures of Alfie. Newborn Alfie, Alfie at his baptism, the playground, taking his first steps and a formal portrait of Alfie and his daddy together. There was one single image of his late wife in a classic silver frame. The wedding photo of him and her together, the two looking hopeful and happy. She was a beautiful woman and Alfie had inherited her blond hair and wide smile. The rest of him was all Cooper. Their baby boy was a beautiful blending of their best physical attributes. Kiely lifted the image from the desktop and studied it intently before returning it to its resting spot. It was evident that Cooper had loved her immensely and that bond hadn't died with her.

Kiely turned her attention to the oversized corkboard that rested on the floor, leaning against the wall beside the desk. Cooper had laid out all the elements of the RevitaYou case. Images of the players, detailed sticky notes and pushpins covered the surface. Pulling up a chair, she took a seat and studied it carefully. Despite the details that they knew being very straightforward, they still had more questions than answers, no closer to putting all the pieces together and closing the case. Even her brother Griffin's fiancée, Abigail—who was also Wes Matthew's estranged daughter—knew nothing.

Clearly, Cooper brought work home with him and she had to wonder how often and how much. Was he a perpetual workaholic, ignoring family and friends during his off time? Was he compromising his relationship with his son, too often focused on bad guys who'd done bad things? Was quality time not necessarily quality because he couldn't let his day job go?

Kiely knew his type and she avoided them like the plague. Men who knew how to work hard but couldn't or wouldn't play hard, too. Men more concerned about their pension than passion, unable to configure the two together in their lives. Men much like her father. Kiely blew a soft sigh.

The renowned Graham Colton had been beloved by all. But his career had sometimes taken precedence over his family. So much so that he rarely noticed how unhappy her mother had been, or he hadn't cared. Sadly, Kiely would never know which. Her mother had sacrificed much for the man she loved, giving up her own dreams of being a social worker to support his career. She'd dedicated her life to her children and her husband, her devotion to them all undeniable.

The last years of their relationship had been strained at best. They were cordial to one another in the presence of others, but behind closed doors, they lived in separate bedrooms and barely spoke. Growing up, Kiely had thought their relationship was perfection, their love for each other so abundant that it sometimes felt unreal. Discovering that it was and watching them slowly unravel until they were a semblance of the fantasy Kiely had made them out to be, was why Kiely avoided any man wanting a serious relationship. Casual encounters and having friends with benefits worked well and she couldn't think of any reason to fix what wasn't broke.

She stole another glance at the photo of Cooper and his wife. Joy shimmered in his blue eyes, his adoration for the woman so abundant that it leapt out of the picture. Kiely had never known that kind of love and didn't imagine that she ever would. But she couldn't help but wonder what that might feel like.

Cooper woke with a start. For a moment he did not know where he was and he sat up abruptly. The pain through his torso was a swift reminder of where he was and what had happened. He had cursed. Loudly. Inhaling air deep into his lungs he took a moment to collect himself, then had thrown his legs over the side of the bed.

The house was quiet. Almost too quiet. When he checked the time, he discovered that he'd been sleeping for almost four hours and was surprised. It had been quite some time since he'd slept so soundly. Before Alfie had been born had probably been one of the last times. He moved into the master bathroom to splash cold water on his face and wipe the sleep from his eyes. After rinsing his mouth with mint-flavored mouthwash, he slipped on a pair of sweatpants. With one last glance in the full-length mirror that hung behind the door, he'd pulled his hand through his hair and eased out of the room.

Alfie's room was his first stop. His son was sleeping soundly, curled in fetal position beneath a flannel blanket. His favorite stuffed bunny and a plastic Tonka truck lay at the foot of the bed with him. The child snored, his mouth open as he sucked air in and blew it out. Cooper brushed his fingers across the kid's forehead. He too seemed to be more relaxed and at ease, sleeping sounder than Cooper remembered having seen him.

Both doors to the bathroom were open, the second bedroom dark. Peeking in to make sure Kiely wasn't there, he felt his stomach flip, concern washing over his spirt. He moved back to the crib, leaning to kiss his son's cheek before he tiptoed out of the room.

He found Kiely sitting in his office, evidently lost in thought. She sat staring into space and he wondered what might be going through her mind. She'd changed, wearing oversized cotton pajamas that swallowed her petite frame. She'd pulled her hair back into a ponytail and fuzzy slippers covered her feet.

He suddenly wondered if asking her to stay with him to help had been a good idea. Because he found himself wondering what it would be like to hold her hand, brush his lips against her cheek and maybe even claim her heart. Thoughts he hadn't entertained about any woman since Sara. Thoughts he had no business contemplating. He suddenly felt a hint of guilt pierce his heart and he shook himself from the trance he'd dropped into. He cleared his throat to draw her attention.

Kiely jumped at the noise, drawing her hand to her chest. She had been so engrossed in her own thoughts that she'd forgotten where she was and what she needed to be doing. She hadn't even considered Cooper might be awake.

He stood in the doorway of the office staring at her and she suddenly felt like she might have been intruding on space where she had no business being. He was also standing there half-naked, wearing only a pair of gray sweatpants. His abs were nearly perfect, his muscles clearly defined. Spending time in a gym had served him well. Him bare-chested, in his bare feet was disconcerting and admittedly, she thought, sexy as hell.

She took a deep breath. "You scared me!"

He smiled. "Sorry about that. You were so focused I wasn't sure if I should interrupt."

"I hope you don't mind that I was in your office." She gestured toward the board. "I was just looking at everything you had on the case."

"No, it's fine. I don't mind at all. Consider this your home while you're here." He pushed both hands into the pockets of the sweats, moving the fabric to tighten around his pelvis.

Kiely tried not to stare. "So, are you hungry? I made dinner."

"You cook?"

"Why do you say that like you're surprised?"

"I am. You've never come across as that Susie homemaker type."

"I'm not, but I can cook. I'm much more than my overwhelming intellect and charming personality, Agent Winston."

Cooper laughed. "Well, I'm starved so let's see if you're any good at it."

Rising from her seat, Kiely moved through the door, brushing past him. "I'll have you know," she said as she shot him a sharp look, "I'm good at everything I do."

In the kitchen she unwrapped the plate that she had set aside for him and popped it into the microwave. Looking around, Cooper saw for the first time, that she had been busy while he slept. The toys that had been scattered around the space had all been put away. The pillows on the sofa had been fluffed and the carpet had been vacuumed. The kitchen was also spotless, the dishes washed and the counters clean.

"Wow!" he said. "You've been busy."

"I had some time after I put Alfie down for the night."

"I'm sorry I missed that," Cooper said. "You must think I'm a horrible father. My son gets kidnapped and I've barely had ten minutes for him since we got him back."

Kiely shrugged her shoulders. "Not really. Now, had you not been shot, I might feel differently." She gestured for him to take a seat at the counter as she set the plate down against the marble countertop.

The aroma of buttered noodles topped with thin slices of ribeye roast seasoned with fresh rosemary, thyme and garlic and a side of peas and carrots suddenly had Cooper salivating. He sat down, grabbed a fork and began to eat. After two bites he nearly purred. "Mmm! This is really good."

Kiely smiled, her lips lifting sweetly. "I told you I could cook."

"Did you have any problems getting my son to eat? He can be very picky. Or he's just tired of franks and beans, which is my specialty."

"Not at all. He ate a nice portion of the noodles, peas and carrots and probably one or two slices of meat. Then we had peaches and ice cream for dessert."

Cooper shook his head. "I'm starting to think I may have gotten the wrong kid back."

"Why would you say that?" Kiely asked, her eyes wide.

"Because Alfie has never been that agreeable about food."

"Alfie's never had my cooking before."

"We might have to keep you!" Cooper said before realizing what that might have sounded like.

Kiely gave him a look but said nothing, instead turning back to the microwave to wipe it down with a damp cloth.

"Out of idle curiosity where did you get the groceries from? It's been a minute since I last went shopping. That had been on my to-do list before Alfie was snatched."

"You do know there are places that will deliver, don't you? You never have to step foot in a grocery store ever again."

"Groceries?" He looked genuinely surprised.

Kiely laughed. She pulled open the refrigerator

door. "Groceries," she responded. "And on a good day, you can get your order within an hour."

Cooper stared at the once-bare refrigerator that was now fully stocked. There was a gallon of fresh milk, a jug of orange juice, eggs, yogurt, an assortment of fresh vegetables and multiple snacks. The freezer was equally stocked and Cooper stared in awe.

"Remember what I said about keeping you?" he said. "I think I may have meant that!"

Kiely laughed.

After Cooper had finished his plate, literally licking it clean, she filled two bowls with a scoop of butter pecan ice cream and peaches that had been oven roasted and then tossed with cinnamon and sugar.

She climbed onto the cushioned stool beside him. Conversation between them flowed like water from a faucet. Kiely discovered his affinity for sweets and his dislike for green vegetables. She shared that she was not a fan of cottage cheese, but potato chips, the lightly salted wavy ones, were her Achilles' heel. They talked about their families. His mother had died years earlier from breast cancer and his father was living in a senior community in Florida. They video chatted weekly but Cooper hoped to take Alfie to visit his grandpop one day.

He offered his condolences for the losses of her parents and listened as she talked about how she and her siblings worked daily to honor their memories. She was close to her siblings and called them her best friends. He was an only child and slightly envious, not knowing what it was like to grow up with family so close. Cooper was impressed with how well-rounded she was, not at all as flighty and reckless as he had once thought.

Almost two hours and a second helping of dessert later, Kiely realized he wasn't wound as tightly as she'd initially thought and he had a keen sense of humor.

"I should head to bed," Kiely said, reaching for his empty plate.

Cooper stopped her, his fingers gently grazing the back of her hand. "I'll clear the dishes. You've done enough. Thank you."

"You're supposed to be resting."

"I don't think putting a plate in the dishwasher will hurt me."

"Well," Kiely said as she stood up, "if it does, don't say I didn't warn you."

He smiled. "I'll keep that in mind. Good night, Kiely."

Her eyes shimmered as she met his stare. Her lips lifted in a bright smile. "Good night, Cooper."

Kiely stared down into the crib as she straightened the blanket around Alfie. She trailed a light hand against his back, patting him gently when he stirred. She found herself in awe of how peacefully he slept. He really was the sweetest little thing, she thought. Everything about him tugged at her heartstrings. She could only begin to imagine the fear Cooper had felt when he'd been missing because she knew that if anything were to happen to him now she'd be beside herself.

If she had to explain her sudden bond with the little boy she didn't know if she had the words. He had somehow wrangled a tight grip on her heart and she was feeling very protective of him. Maybe her sisters were wrong, Kiely thought, and her maternal instincts had simply been late to bloom.

She gave the baby monitor one last check to ensure it was on and at full volume. Moving through the shared bathroom to the other bedroom she sat down on the edge of the bed. It had been a nice evening. She'd enjoyed her time with Cooper. He'd been easy to talk to and had even made her laugh a time or two. She liked him more than she had expected and liking Cooper Winston had never been part of her plans.

Slipping beneath the covers, Kiely settled down against the pillows. She pulled an arm up and over her head, her other hand playing with the buttons on her pajama top. She hoped that thoughts of Cooper weren't going to haunt her dreams, but she had a feeling she wasn't going to be able to get him out of her head anytime soon.

# Chapter 5

The next morning when Cooper woke he was surprised by the late hour. He was also surprised that he had not heard Alfie because the youngster would usually have been crying for something to eat by now. Then he remembered he had turned off the baby monitor and his heart dropped into the pit of his stomach.

Jumping from the bed he made quick work of his morning routine and headed straight for the nursery. He found the crib empty and for a moment he panicked, hurrying toward the family room.

Alfie and Kiely were together. She sat cross-legged and they were playing a game of peekaboo.

The toddler ran in circles around her as she pretended to cover her eyes and then surprise him over and over again. The little boy exploded with laughter every time she uncovered her eyes and said *boo*.

"Good morning," Cooper said. He gave them a wave of his hand.

"Dad-dy!" Alfie rushed forward, throwing himself into Cooper's arms.

"Don't lift him!" Kiely admonished, though her words fell on deaf ears. She shook her head and smiled. Cooper knew he'd conveniently forgotten, or had chosen to ignore, his doctor's orders. But Alfie's smile was well worth it.

Cooper lifted his son up toward the ceiling and spun them both in a circle. He brought him close and kissed his face. "Good morning, Alfie!"

"Alfie playing with Ki-Ki!" the child responded. He pointed toward Kiely.

"We're still practicing my name," Kiely said with a soft giggle. "I think Ki-Ki might be it for now."

Cooper laughed. His son's delight was infectious, and the little boy was completely smitten with Kiely. Almost as smitten as he himself was if he were honest. Watching the two together tickled Cooper's spirit, sparking joy he hadn't felt in some time. "You two are up early."

"Actually, I think you might be late. In fact, I'm pretty sure of it. We've been up for a while."

He nodded. "I don't know if I can get used to this

rest thing. And it's taking me a minute to get used to someone else being in the house taking care of Alfie. I panicked for a minute when he wasn't in his room."

Alfie kicked to be put down and ran back to Kiely. He threw his little arms around her neck and hugged her.

"Snack time!" she chimed as she stood up, Alfie still hanging onto her back as she grabbed his legs for a piggyback ride. "And breakfast for Daddy."

"Don't worry about me. I usually only have coffee."

"Don't you know that breakfast is the most important meal of the day? You need to be setting an example for your son."

"I barely have time to feed him in the mornings before it's time to head to day care."

"Let me guess, you work until the wee hours of the morning and then you barely get a decent night's sleep before you need to be up doing it all over again?"

"Ding! Ding! Ding!" he said facetiously. "And you win the prize!"

Kiely laughed. "It's a good thing I'm here to help you figure out how to do better."

He gave her a wry smile but didn't respond.

"Come sit," Kiely commanded, pointing to an empty chair at the table. She placed Alfie into his booster seat and secured the safety straps.

By the time Cooper made it to the table to sit down, Kiely was placing bowls of freshly cut fruit on the table mats before him and Alfie. Alfie immediately grabbed an apple slice in one fist and two large red grapes in the other.

She moved back to the stovetop and turned on the burner. By the time Cooper was done with his fruit, she'd prepared him a croissant sandwich with honey-baked ham, a fried egg and melted brie. She placed his plate on the table with a cup of freshly brewed coffee and then her own.

The faintest sliver of melancholy swept over Cooper. He couldn't help but think how things might have been for him and Alfie had Sarah lived. How differently his son's life would be if his mother had been there to cut fruit for his breakfast and rock him to sleep at night. He shook the emotion away, turning his attention back to Kiely. "You didn't eat breakfast?"

She shrugged. "I wanted to wait for you. I cooked oatmeal for Alfie and fed him and then he and I played until you woke up."

"You cooked oatmeal? And Alfie ate it?"

"He loved it. It's one of my best recipes. You cook the oats and you can do them in the microwave or on the stovetop. After they're done you slowly stir in some egg whites for added protein. It also makes them super creamy. Then I add some coconut oil and cinnamon. Those are great immunity boosters and I'm told kids can never have too many. Then I top them with chocolate chips and raspberries, which Alfie loved. Sometimes when I make it I'll do nut butter or nuts, or toasted coconut and pineapple."

"That actually sounds pretty good and I'm not a fan of oatmeal."

"I'll make you some this week and you can give it a try," she said. "I'll have you eating healthy in no time."

Cooper held up the last bite of his ham and brie. "I imagine this isn't wholeheartedly healthy but it's very good."

"Thank you." She reached over to wipe Alfie's hands with a napkin. He'd eaten the last piece of cantaloupe from the bowl and the juice had run down his arm. She turned back to Cooper. "So, what's on your agenda today?"

"I need to get back to work. I need to solve this case."

Kiely nodded. "Well, first things first. You and Alfie need some quality daddy and son time. Why don't you read him a story or two while I clean up and then after you put him down for his nap, we can do some work so we can solve this case," she said, emphasizing the *we*.

Cooper gave her a bright smile, feeling amusement dance across his face. There was an edge to Kiely that he found exhilarating. There were moments of softness, too, that he saw when she engaged with Alfie. Then there was that take-charge, work-hard, no-nonsense side of her that didn't play. That side was commanding, demanding and quite engaging. "Yes, ma'am!" He lifted Alfie from his seat and nuzzled his cheek against his son's. "Kiely said it's story time, kiddo!"

Alfie threw his hands in the air and laughed. "Ki-Ki!"

An hour or so later when Cooper returned from putting Alfie down for his nap, his doorbell rang. He and Kiely exchanged a look.

"Were you expecting someone?" Kiely asked as she moved to the cupboard and reached for the revolver that she had hidden behind a bag of sugar. She checked the chamber and slid it into the back waistband of her pants.

Cooper shook his head as he disappeared into his office. When he came back he was checking the chamber of his service weapon. Kiely watched him as he moved to the front door. After peering out through the peephole first, he took a step back then secured his gun in the waistband of his pants. He tossed her another look before pulling the door open. Tripp McKellar and Emmanuel Iglesias stood sheepishly on the other side.

"Good morning," Emmanuel said. "I hope this isn't a bad time?"

"Not at all," Cooper answered. "Come in." He stepped back to let both men enter the home.

"Hey, there!" Kiely greeted. She gave them a slight wave. "What brings the dynamic duo by this morning?"

Emmanuel's eyes widened at the sight of her. "Kiely! This is a surprise. I wasn't expecting to find you here," he said.

"On the job. Cooper needed help after he got out of the hospital," she answered.

He nodded. "Pippa didn't mention it."

"Bad Pippa," she said sarcastically.

Cooper laughed. "Kiely's been a big help, especially with Alfie."

Emmanuel eyed her with a raised brow and a smug smile. Kiely could already see him racing back to her sister to tattle as if she and Pippa didn't already share everything. She rolled her eyes skyward.

"Can I get you two a cup of coffee?" Kiely questioned, turning an about-face.

"No, thank you," Tripp answered. "We're not staying. I wanted to check on your security detail outside and make sure everything was going okay."

"We also had some news to share," Emmanuel added.

"Good news, I hope," said Cooper. He gestured for the two of them to have a seat at the kitchen table.

Emmanuel shook his head. "It's Gunther Johnson. He's changed his mind about giving up the goods on Capital X."

"He's scared," Tripp said. "We think someone may have gotten to him."

Cooper shook his head. Kiely threw up her hands in frustration. Both were all too familiar with the career criminal. Gunther Johnson had been a hired enforcer for Capital X, the private loan operation whose seedy, underground lending operation preyed on borrowers with astronomical interest rates, substantial loan fees and shady collection practices. Known to respond with threats and violence if payments were missed, they had been on the law enforcement radar for some time.

Brody had borrowed fifty thousand dollars from Capital X to invest in RevitaYou. Wes Matthews had absconded with his money shortly after. When Brody was unable to make his repayment, Capital X had sent Gunther Johnson to break two of his fingers, promising to break two more if he didn't come up with the money he owed. Capital X's henchmen chasing him was the reason why Brody had disappeared.

Weeks earlier Pippa had helped with the sting operation to take down Capital X and its owners. Gunther Johnson had been caught in that sting but had been less than cooperative. Working out a deal with the district attorney, he'd finally agreed to give up the Capital X hierarchy and name who oversaw the operation. To now hear he was refusing to talk didn't sit well with any of them.

"We need that name," Cooper snapped, his irritation clouding his good mood. "That name might get us closer to Wes Matthews."

"I spoke to the DA and he said he was going to contact you. I filled him in on the shooting so he said he was going to give you a day or two before he called," Tripp said.

"I'll call him as soon as we're done. I need to go see him," Cooper said, "to see how he plans to play this." He shot a quick glance in Kiely's direction, expecting a comment but none came.

"Just take care of yourself," Emmanuel said, rising. "We'll check back in with you and you know if you need anything all you have to do is call." He extended his hand to shake Cooper's.

"Thank you. I appreciate you guys stopping by."

"We're here if you need us," Tripp reiterated as they moved toward the door. "But I'm sure you're in good hands." He gestured with his head toward Kiely, winked his eye at her and smiled.

Kiely smiled and Cooper was ready for him to be gone. He looked at her and then Tripp and back at her. He took two steps to his right, as if moving to block Tripp's view of her.

"Yes," Cooper said. "I definitely am." He tossed a look over his shoulder.

Kiely laughed. And Cooper tightened his jaw,

raising his brows. He practically threw the two men out the door, keeping his goodbyes short and swift.

"You're funny," she said.

"What?"

"I see how you act every time Tripp is around."

"I don't know what you're talking about." He double-checked the door lock one last time, feigning disinterest in her comment.

"If I didn't know better I'd think you were a little jealous," she said teasingly.

Cooper turned away from her, moving toward his office. "I don't get jealous."

She laughed again. "Not much you don't," she muttered under her breath.

He stopped in the doorway and it was on the tip of his tongue to ask if she were interested in the man, but he didn't. He didn't want to know the answer if by chance she said yes. He said instead, "I need to call the DA," and then he disappeared into the other room, closing the door behind himself.

# Chapter 6

The next day, the Uber driver would not stop talking and his incessant drone was beginning to wear on Cooper's last good nerve. Using a ride-share service had not been his choice. He had wanted to drive himself to the district attorney's office. Kiely had no issues with him going but she'd been adamant about how he got there. Since she needed to watch Alfie and couldn't drive him herself, Uber had been her idea and he had acquiesced to stall the argument brewing between them. She'd issued a host of threats she promised to rain down on him had he gotten into his car to drive himself and none of them had been pretty.

Kiely Colton was spit and fire when she wanted to make a point and she'd had a few to make about him not following doctor's orders. Had this meeting not been important he would have crawled back into bed as she had wanted because he hurt. He hurt more than he wanted to admit—and he would never admit that to Kiely.

His first stop was the Kent County Prosecutor's Office. The district attorney of record was Eugene Beckwith. Eugene and Cooper had worked many cases together and he was highly respected amongst his peers. He rarely sugarcoated things and could often be bitterly blunt. Cooper appreciated that he always knew where the man stood on an issue.

Eugene rushed in his direction, visibly irritated. "It's good to see you, Agent Winston. I was surprised when you called. I got the impression you were going to be off your feet for a minute."

"I probably should be, but duty calls."

Eugene nodded. "Detective Iglesias said he updated you?"

"He did. Emmanuel indicated Gunther Johnson is recanting his earlier statements and wants to forfeit his deal with the state."

"That dirtbag is playing us. Personally, I don't think what he claims to know is as big as he wanted us to believe. Now he's got cold feet because he can't deliver. I know you need that information, but Johnson's looking at life in prison, no matter what he does. Whether or not we make that time comfortable for him doesn't much matter to me. Like I don't already have a dozen other cases to worry about. No one has time for this!"

"I agree, but we still need to try. I want to talk to him."

Eugene shrugged. "It's your time to waste. How soon are you looking?"

"I'd like to head over there right now."

"Give me a second to contact his attorney," the man said. He stepped away, pulling his cell phone to his ear. A few short minutes later he moved back to Cooper's side. He nodded. "You're good to go. His attorney will meet you at the jail in one hour."

Cooper and the man shook hands. "Thank you," Cooper said.

"I'd say good luck, but you'll need more than luck to deal with that con artist."

Cooper smirked. "I appreciate your faith in my abilities."

The Grand Rapids city jail was Cooper's second stop. The building at Monroe Center NW was a holding facility for the Grand Rapids Police Department and agencies within the judicial district of Kent County. Its proximity to the courthouse and the county clerk's office made for easy visits when needed.

When Cooper arrived, the jailer on duty took

him directly to an interrogation room to wait. For twenty minutes he sat twiddling his thumbs, trying to decide how he planned to appeal to the criminal and sway his decision. When the defense attorney entered, looking slightly flustered, Cooper found himself whispering a quick prayer that this didn't prove to be harder than necessary.

The door swung open a second time and a guard walked Gunther Johnson into the room. Although Cooper had seen photos of the man—multiple mug shots, a high school yearbook image, and a picture captured on a nearby security camera when he'd been arrested—he was struck by Gunther's physique. He had a sizeable build, bald head and cold, ice-blue eyes. He was intimidating, looking like brute force beneath his ivory complexion.

Gunther gave his lawyer a narrow stare, then dropped heavily onto the wood chair. He leaned back in the seat as he shifted his gaze toward Cooper.

Cooper leaned forward in his own seat, folding his hands together atop the table. "Mr. Johnson, I'm FBI Agent Cooper Winston. I'm here to talk to you about your deal with the DA to give up the name of your Capital X associates."

"I'm not taking no deal. I told them that," he spat, annoyance furrowing his brow. "I changed my mind."

"May I ask why?"

"It's none of your business."

"Let me keep it real with you, Mr. Johnson. We need that name."

"And my client needs a safety net or that can't happen," the attorney interjected.

"I ain't talking!" Gunther reiterated, his lips forming a petulant pout like he was in kindergarten.

"The district attorney has been very generous with his offer to you."

"Is he going to let me off? Give me…what's that they call it…immunity…that's it…full immunity?"

"Be real, Mr. Johnson. The district attorney has an airtight case against you for murder, and I'm sure if the FBI does a little more digging we can probably link you to a few others. You'd be looking at the death penalty for certain, instead of a cushy life sentence."

"The death penalty?" Gunther shot his attorney a look. "You ain't said nothing about no death penalty!"

The man waved a dismissive hand. "Because the state of Michigan abolished capital punishment. He's just blowing smoke!"

Cooper smiled. "But Indiana and Ohio do and I'm sure it won't take much to tie you to Capital X customers in both states. Let me see," Cooper said as he flipped open the manila folder in front of him.

He continued. "Paul Phelps, a resident of Gary, Indiana, found dead with four fingers missing. Regina Leslie, also a resident of Gary. Jon Tucker of Columbus, Ohio. They all borrowed money from Capital X. They all had problems repaying. And what else do they have in common? You. You traveled to both states around the time of their murders. That sounds like a death penalty case to me. Crossing state lines means an interagency investigation."

"You said no death penalty!" Gunther shouted at his attorney, although he was staring at Cooper.

Cooper smirked. "Well, now I'm saying I'm sure my office will have no qualms pushing a death penalty agenda for the time you've wasted yanking our chain!" He slammed the file folder closed.

"He will kill me if I tell!"

"Who, Mr. Johnson?"

"You can't protect me!" He was shouting, still visibly agitated.

The guard by the door took a step forward. Cooper held up his hand to stall him.

"Yes, we can," Cooper said. "The DA laid out a plan that would guarantee your protection. He's agreed to protecting your identity and sending you to a prison facility where you wouldn't be recognized."

"And my television?"

"If he promised you that, he'll honor it. But you have to do what you promised to do."

Gunther leaned over to whisper into his attorney's ear. The two men whispered back and forth for a few good minutes before Gunther turned back to Cooper. "I'm just not sure."

Cooper stood up. "You have twenty-four hours, Mr. Johnson, or the DA's offer is off the table and then I promise to personally make your life a living hell." He gave the attorney one last look. "Twenty-four hours and that's being very generous."

The Uber ride back put Cooper smack dab in the middle of evening traffic. The driver was regaling him with a story about his bachelor party antics in Brazil, where every woman with a tan and a bikini apparently wanted him. The man was hardly ready for marriage, Cooper thought. Marriage required a commitment of time and thought that few were prepared for. Marriage was about shared space and goals and sometimes stepping back from your own dreams for someone else to fly. He'd been there and done that, albeit not as well as he probably should have.

He had never been able to apologize to Sara for sometimes being selfish and self-absorbed. He often thought about the apology she had deserved from him when a case or a client had his full attention and she had felt taken for granted. Parenting Alfie had taught him much about himself. He hadn't been the man his wife had deserved but he was determined to be a better man for his son.

They were stopped at a light and Casanova Junior was still going on about some blonde with big boobs. Cooper stared out the window, his thoughts on Alfie, and on Kiely. He was still in awe of how quickly Alfie had become attached to the woman. To see them together one would think she'd been in his short little life since forever, Kiely mothering him as if he were her own. He also had to wonder what would happen when the time came for Kiely to leave them. How would Alfie handle her not being there. Because they couldn't keep her around indefinitely. No matter how much he suddenly found himself wanting to.

Kiely knew she was butchering the words to the lullaby that she was singing, but Alfie didn't seem to mind. She held him in her arms, his head resting on her chest, his little legs wrapped around her waist. She rocked him from side to side and he was slowly drifting off to sleep.

Her voice was a loud whisper as she sang. "The other night dear, as I lay sleeping, I dreamt I held you, up in my arms. But when I woke, dear, I was mistaken, so hmm hmmm hmm hmmm and cried."

She kissed his little forehead as his eyes finally closed, his little body relaxing against her. "You are my sunshine, my only sunshine. You make me happy when skies are gray! You'll never know dear, how much I love you. Please don't take my sunshine away."

She hummed for a few more minutes until she was certain he was sound asleep. Then she laid him gently in his crib. Everything about Alfie was joy. Kiely still couldn't fathom how quickly he'd captured a huge chunk of her heart. She was loving every minute of her time with the child. When Alfie had wakened from his afternoon nap Cooper was already headed to his meeting. She'd devoted the entire afternoon to the little boy's entertainment. They'd played hokey pokey, pick-up sticks, rolled a ball, played with slime, had two snacks, a bubble bath and now he was past the point of exhaustion. Admittedly, so was she. Kiely was quickly discovering that kids required an abundance of energy she had not anticipated.

She was still staring down at the little boy when she heard Cooper arrive home. She turned to see him watching her from the doorway. He moved into the room to stand beside her. She was only slightly startled when his arm brushed against her shoulder.

"Hey! I didn't hear you come in!"

"I haven't been here long. I stopped to chat with Officer Parnell. He's watching the house tonight. He said things have been quiet since he came on duty."

"It's been very uneventful."

"How long has Alfie been asleep?"

"About thirty minutes. He's just the sweetest angel when he's sleeping."

Cooper smiled. "He really is!"

Folding her arms across her chest Kiely bumped his side with her hip. "Hungry?"

"I could eat."

"Good. I'm starved and I waited to eat with you."

"You didn't have to wait!"

"I know that." She bumped his side a second time as she turned to exit the room.

"Do I have time to take a quick shower?"

Kiely nodded. "We're eating salmon. I'll put it in the oven when I hear the water shut off."

He gently tapped her arm. "Thank you, Kiely."

Kiely pulled the orange and honey-glazed salmon from the oven. The dining table had been set for two and she was ready to eat. She plated their meals and set the food on the table. Dinner was the salmon, a mushroom and spinach salad, rice pilaf, and a whipped chocolate mousse for dessert.

When another ten minutes passed and there was no sign of Cooper, Kiely eased her way down the hallway to his bedroom door. The door was cracked open and peeking through she saw Cooper standing in the center of the room. He wore a pair of boxer briefs, nothing more. His skin was flushed from the shower's hot water. He stood slathering his body with lotion, his hands gliding across his torso and up and down his limbs. Her eyes widened at the sight of him. He was a beautiful specimen of manhood and Kiely gasped, feeling heat course straight through her feminine spirit. She took two steps back, and one very big inhale of air, and then she called his name.

"Cooper? Dinner's ready!"

"Coming!" Cooper called back.

As Kiely moved back down the hallway, the bedroom door swung open and Cooper hurried after her. He had slipped on another pair of sweatpants and a T-shirt with the FBI logo on his chest.

"Sorry about that," Cooper said. "Emmanuel called to say Gunther Johnson is ready to talk."

"That's great! I guess you ignoring the doctor's orders was worth it," Kiely said, an air of attitude in her tone.

Cooper laughed. "Are you really going to give me a hard time about leaving?"

"Would I do something like that?" Kiely responded as she pulled her hand to her chest and batted her lashes at him.

"You have jokes!" He pulled the chair out for her and they both sat down to eat.

"How do you feel?" Kiely questioned.

"Better, now."

"So, will you have to go back tomorrow?"

"I don't think so, but we'll see. I'll know more in the morning."

"I'm just glad you convinced him to talk."

There was an awkward silence that suddenly settled over the table.

Kiely's gaze narrowed as she studied his expression. "What?"

Cooper lifted his eyes to hers. "I bluffed. I told him I had information that could possibly get him the death penalty." He gave her a blow-by-blow of his conversation with Gunther.

"And he fell for it?"

Cooper nodded. "It would seem so if he's ready to talk."

"Sounds like you might need to do some serious investigating. Clearly, he's been involved in some things we don't even know about yet."

"That's what I was thinking, too!"

"Well, if he talks, then the lie was well worth it. Sometimes you have to do whatever you have to do."

Cooper processed her comment. Skirting the rules by lying to get information wasn't something he ever did and he found himself feeling out of sorts about his actions. Although what he'd done was well within the scope of the law, it went against his personal moral code. He also found it interesting that Kiely hadn't blinked an eye, not at all bothered by what he had done.

"I've been thinking about Alfie's kidnapping. Going through all the players we know to try and figure out who could have done it," Kiely said.

"Well, we know a man snatched him. So, he and that woman at the cabin were working together."

Kiely nodded. "And both are somehow affiliated with Wes Matthews."

"What about family? There's his daughter, Abigail."

"It's certainly not her. Abigail and my brother Griffin are an item. She barely knows her father. Her mother left her father when she was a child. It was Abigail who helped uncover the ricin in Revita-You. She wants to see him caught more than anyone."

"So, refresh my memory. Griffin is the attorney?"

"Yes. He specializes in adoption law."

"But he's not the only attorney in the family. Right?"

"That's right. My sister Victoria is a JAG paralegal and my twin sister Pippa is also a lawyer."

"Interesting."

"Why interesting?"

"It just is. But we digress." He took a sip of his wine and then refilled his crystal goblet. "So, we can eliminate Wes's daughter Abigail. And you said her mother is deceased, right? So, who else is there in his life that would want to protect him?"

Kiely shrugged. "Abigail said her father has dated a few women that she knows about."

Kiely leaned back in her seat. "What I find interesting is that the kidnapper called you specifically. And that she took Alfie. When you consider all the agencies working this case, all looking for Matthews in some form or fashion, why did she single you out to contact? Why your son? It makes me question if maybe she has some personal connection to you."

"I'm at a loss as to who it could be," Cooper said after a minute of contemplation.

Kiely continued. "I also keep thinking about the tip that came in over that hotline. Someone knew Wes Matthews had a connection to that property."

"Do you think they knew about my baby being there?"

"Good question. Wish I had an answer for you. Hopefully the info Gunther gives you will lead us all farther along on this case."

Kiely rose from the table and began to clear the dishes.

"Let me help with that," Cooper said as he lifted his own plate from the table. "Dinner was excellent tonight, by the way."

"Thank you."

She brushed against him as they passed each other. Heat blossomed between them like the sweetest breeze. "Excuse me," she muttered.

"No problem." Cooper moved to the sink and began to wash the dishes. He tossed a dry towel in her direction. "So, did you and Alfie have a good day?" Cooper asked, changing the subject.

"We had a great day," Kiely answered.

"May I ask you a personal question?" Cooper asked.

"I guess that depends on how personal the question is," Kiely said with a soft giggle. "But ask away."

"I was just wondering why you never married. Why don't you have any kids? You're so good with them. I would think that you would want to have children of your own."

Kiely laughed, the wealth of it gut deep.

"Why is that so funny?" Cooper questioned.

"Because I really have never had a lot of experience with kids. In fact, I never imagined myself having children. My sisters have always said that I don't have any maternal instincts whatsoever."

"Well, obviously your sisters got that wrong! You really are a natural."

"I'll be honest. It's really surprised me how much I enjoy taking care of Alfie. He's definitely a handful but I adore him."

"Well, I appreciate just how good you are with him."

"Have you ever thought about remarrying?" Kiely asked casually. "I mean, has there been anyone in your life that would be a great mother figure for Alfie?"

Cooper shrugged. "I've not dated much since my wife died." He gave her a quick look.

"I don't date much either," Kiely said. "Colton Investigations keeps me busy."

"So, you put work before everything else, too."

"I have. But my time with Alfie, and with you, has me rethinking what my future should look like. And don't get me wrong, I have a great life. But I've been happier these past two days than I've been in a very long while."

She gave him a slight smile, her demure expression hitting Cooper like a gut punch he wasn't expecting. He bit down against his bottom lip. His body's reaction was purely carnal, a rise of nature suddenly twitching for attention. He felt heat flush his cheeks. Kiely turned to put the dishes back into the cupboard, apparently pretending not to notice, as he turned his back to her, needing to adjust himself in his pants.

"Well," he said as he turned back. He reached for another bottle of wine, pulled two clean glasses from the rack, and poured. He passed one glass to her, then extended his in a mock toast. "Here's to embarrassing myself," he said as he clinked his glass against hers.

Kiely laughed. "That sounds very personal."

Cooper took a large swig of his drink.

"You do know you're not supposed to mix your pain pills with alcohol, right?"

"I won't tell if you don't."

"Cooper Winston, you know better!"

He shrugged. "I think you're rubbing off on me. I'm wanting to take more risks than usual."

"So, try skydiving. It's so much safer!"

He laughed, his joy rising abundantly. He was suddenly staring into her eyes as she watched him, the coy look on her face giving him pause. He rested his glass on the counter and took a step closer to her. Kiely's eyes widened, her lips parting ever so slightly. Her perfume wafted to his nostrils and her body heat felt like the sweetest caress as it rose with a vengeance between them. He found himself staring at her mouth, wondering what she might taste like, suddenly wanting to kiss her lips, to tease her with his tongue as he held her in his arms. He wanted her like a thirsty man did water.

"Kiely, with everything going on this may not be the right time," he started, "but I really like…"

Before Cooper could finish his statement, the room suddenly shook, something exploding outside. The loud boom was followed by a whooshing sound and the noise of shattering glass as the windows shook.

Instinctively, Cooper reached for Kiely, pulling her to the floor as he wrapped his arms protectively around her. The smell of sulfur dioxide hit their noses, pungent and thick, followed by Alfie's mournful wail.

"You okay?" Cooper asked, his hands clutching Kiely's shoulders as he looked her up and down.

She nodded. "I need to get Alfie," she said as she jumped up, racing down the hallway. "You check outside!"

Cooper went for his weapon, checking the chamber as he moved to the front door. Before he could pull it open, a second explosion blew a hole where the entrance was, knocking him backwards into the wall. He scampered back onto his feet. He screamed Kiely's and Alfie's names.

"We're okay!" she screamed back as Alfie cried hysterically. "Are you okay?"

"Stay inside!" Cooper responded. He moved back to the entrance and peered outside. Across the street the police patrol car was an amalgamation of burned metal, fire and smoke. His own car was nothing but melted shrapnel and Kiely's vehicle, parked behind his, was also engulfed in flames.

Moving to the middle of the yard he looked up the street and then down. His neighbors were peeking out their windows, some beginning to come out of their homes to see what had happened. In the distance, the faint sound of sirens could be heard rushing toward them. He looked toward the police vehicle a second time and his stomach pitched, bile rising into his throat. He bent forward at the waist, fighting not to vomit.

"Agent Winston!" A voice called his name from the side of the house.

Cooper turned abruptly, his weapon raised. He

dropped it just as quickly. "Officer Parnell, thank God!" Cooper exclaimed. He rushed to meet the man, throwing his arms around him in a bear hug. Relief flooded his spirit, easing the knot that had tightened in his belly. "I was afraid you were still in that car."

"No, sir. Thank the good Lord! I thought I saw someone moving along the side of your home and I'd gotten out to investigate. That second blast knocked me on my ass, but I'm okay. Backup is already on the way. You good, sir?"

Cooper glanced toward the front door of his home. Kiely stood in the entrance, Alfie clutched tightly to her. She gave him a nod of her head as she pressed her lips to his son's forehead. "We're good," he said, shifting his gaze back to the other man.

The cell phone in Cooper's pocket suddenly rang. He pulled it to his ear, exasperation in his voice. "Hello?"

"You won't be so lucky next time," the woman on the other end spat. Cooper recognized her voice. It was the same woman who'd called after Alfie had been taken. "Who is this?" he snapped.

"Stop looking for Wes Matthews or I won't miss the next time," she said and then she disconnected the call.

Cooper tightened his fist around the device. Whoever she was, this latest rogue move had gotten his full attention. It was only by the grace of God that there had been no serious casualties. But she had now hit him twice. Hard. If he hadn't been certain before, he was now. He would have to change his tactics to catch this woman. Playing by the rules didn't apply when it came to his son and his home. He hurried back to Kiely's side. "Our kidnapper is now an arsonist," he said. "And that was a murder attempt. Parnell got lucky."

Her eyes widened as she reflected on what could have happened to them all. "We got lucky, too," she interjected. "She doesn't plan on stopping, does she?"

"No, which is why we need to find her and find her fast."

# Chapter 7

Thirty minutes after the explosion Grand Rapids police officials had cordoned off Cooper's street, firemen had put out the flames, and agents from the FBI district office were assessing the damage. Investigative teams from each agency were processing the scene and asking questions. Cooper's home had become command central, uniformed officers and suited agents walking in and out of the open door.

Alfie was wide-eyed and curious, trying to comprehend all the excitement. He clung to Kiely as if his life depended on it. She, Cooper and Officer Parnell had each relayed their memory of the event multiple times. One of Cooper's neighbors reported seeing a figure dressed all in black cutting through her yard on a motorcycle.

Emmanuel, Tripp and Agent Claire Miller arrived like the cavalry, each barking orders. Kiely was feeding Alfie orange slices as Cooper filled them in on the phone call.

"We're trying to trace it now!" Tripp said.

Claire shrugged. "If it's a burner, you won't get anything."

"Anything on the traffic cams?" Cooper asked.

"Nothing," Emmanuel said, shaking his head.

"Who is this woman?" Cooper snapped, tossing his hands up in frustration.

"We will get her," Claire said. "For now, though, I think you should stay at the safe house." She looked at Cooper. "We have that one spot you used for your witness protection case last year. It hasn't been put back into available inventory yet. Your stay will be off the books so if this woman is somehow affiliated with the agency she won't be able to find you through us. The only people who will know where you are will be me, Lieutenant Tripp and anyone you choose to tell."

"You don't think she's with the FBI, do you?" Kiely questioned.

Claire shrugged her narrow shoulders. "FBI, CIA, local law enforcement, mercenary training, who knows. She just seems to be good at what she does, so until we figure out who she is, we can't be too careful. I'd rather we be safe now than sorry later."

Cooper nodded. "That'll work."

"We'll make arrangements for your transportation."

"I can help with that," Tripp said. He began punching a message into his smartphone.

"A safe house?" Kiely looked concerned. "I can't just up and disappear," she said. "The case... My work..."

"You can work remotely," Claire volunteered. "It's a state-of-the-art facility with secure Wi-Fi and all the perks of a five-star hotel. You won't even know you're being protected."

Cooper eased over to her side, leaning to whisper in her ear. "I will understand if you don't want to do this, Kiely. I need to make sure Alfie is safe, but this is not your problem. She's after me, not you."

"Do you not *want* me to go with you?" Kiely whispered back. Her eyes skated back and forth across his face, as if searching for something that had yet to be defined or spoken.

He leaned closer, his hand resting against her waist. "I *need* you to go with me," he said. "And I want you to *want* to come."

Kiely nodded her head, her cheek brushing gently against his. Alfie giggled, reaching for his father. Lifting the child from her arms, Cooper gave her a caressing smile and nuzzled his face into the boy's neck.

\* \* \*

Kiely was in the master bedroom packing a suitcase for Cooper and Alfie when Sadie and Pippa barged into the room. The sisters all gave each other a look.

Pippa moved swiftly to her twin sister's side, punched her in the arm and then threw her arms around Kiely's shoulders. "You scared the hell out of me!" she exclaimed.

Kiely laughed as she hugged her sister back. When they finally let go, she rubbed the bruise rising against her skin. "Ouch! That hurt."

"You deserved it."

"I swear! Does that fiancé of yours tell you everything?"

"Emmanuel didn't tell me this."

"Well, how did…" Kiely started.

Sadie waved a hand. "Guilty! Lieutenant McKellar called me in."

"You're investigating?"

Sadie shook her head. "Transport. I'm taking you and your new family to the FBI safe house. He and Agent Miller thought you'd feel better about going if one of us took you."

"Well, isn't that special," Kiely said. "All we need now is Vikki to show up!"

"Don't think we didn't call her," Sadie said. "She didn't answer her phone. She was in court today on a case. But I'm sure we'll hear from her later."

"So, this is where you've been *working*!" Pippa said. She sat down on the edge of the bed and began rifling through the suitcase her sister was packing. "And I assume these belong to your *employer*?" She held up a pair of black boxer briefs.

"Why are you packing for him?" Sadie questioned. "Are things like that between you two now, or is something wrong with his hands?"

Kiely rolled her eyes. "Someone tried to blow him up tonight. I'm just being helpful. Besides, Agent Miller is rushing us to get out of here and he's trying to tie up strings out there. It just made sense for me to help."

"You haven't slept with him, have you?" Pippa questioned.

"I have not slept with him."

Pippa's gaze narrowed. She gave her sister a smile. "But you want to!" she said excitedly.

Kiely held up her index finger. "Shh! Don't let him hear you!"

"I told you she liked him!" Sadie interjected.

There was a knock on the door. When Cooper opened it to peer inside, Alfie came running in, throwing himself at Kiely.

"Ki-Ki!" the little boy exclaimed as she swept him up into her arms. He gave the two sisters a look, staring at Pippa for a good few minutes. The family genes were strong and although she and her sister were fraternal twins they still bore a strong resemblance to one another.

"This is Alfie," Kiely said, making the introductions. "And this is his father, Cooper Winston. Cooper, this is Philippa, my twin, and my sister Sadie."

"It's a pleasure to meet you both," Cooper said. "I wish it was under better circumstances."

"Please, call me Pippa, and the pleasure is mine."

"Nice meeting you," Sadie added. "Isn't this sweet baby just a little doll! Hello there!"

Alfie was still staring at the two. He finally lifted his hand in a slight wave. "Hi! My name Alfie!" he said as he patted his chest proudly.

"Hi, Alfie," Pippa said, teasing his chubby cheek.

"I didn't mean to interrupt, but we need to get going," Cooper said. "I came to see if you needed any help. And I really appreciate you helping me out."

"I'm ready," Kiely answered. She snatched his undergarment from her sister's hand and tossed it back into the suitcase. "We're all packed."

Kiely appreciated her sisters not giving her a hard time, although she knew it would only be a matter of time before they did. The ride to the safe house was taking them through some heavily wooded areas as they headed about an hour's ride out of the Grand Rapids city limits.

Alfie sat in Kiely's lap, her seat belt wrapped

securely around them both. His car seat had been collateral damage in the explosion, nothing but a blob of melted plastic. Sadie had promised to bring another when she came back to check on them.

Sadie drove, she and Pippa sitting in the front. Kiely and Cooper sat in the back with the baby. Nestled shoulder to shoulder the nearness of him gave her an abundance of comfort. His concern for her well-being had been admirable. She appreciated him wanting her opinion and asking her thoughts on what they should do and how they should proceed. His concerns had mirrored her own and he'd had no reservations expressing them.

Pippa tossed her a look from the front seat, her smile slightly smug. Kiely rolled her eyes and her twin laughed.

"You look good with a baby in your arms," Pippa said.

Sadie chuckled. "And a man by your side."

"She does," Cooper answered, a wide grin across his face.

Kiely sat up straighter, adjusting the hold she had around Alfie. He'd fallen back to sleep before they'd passed the first stop light and had been slumbering comfortably the entire ride. "My sisters can't wait to have kids," Kiely said. "And Sadie's fiancé has vowed to impregnate her the minute she says I do."

Pippa laughed. "Tate would impregnate her now

if he thought our brothers wouldn't kill him. Because they would kill him!"

Sadie scoffed. "Let's not bore Agent Winston with our family drama, please."

Kiely laughed, Cooper chuckling with them. She leaned her head against his shoulder and when she did, Cooper gave her knee a light squeeze.

The FBI safe house was a stunning log home nestled in a forest of mature sugar maple and red oak trees. It boasted a covered porch, large deck, landscaped firepit area and a walkout basement. As Cooper carried their luggage inside and checked that all was well before her sisters pulled off, Kiely was already planning excursions for the three of them when safety allowed.

"It looks very pretty," Sadie said. "I wouldn't mind being locked away up here with a handsome man."

"Any handsome man in particular?" Kiely asked.

"She definitely doesn't want to be stuck up here with Tate," Pippa muttered.

"Now you're just being mean," Sadie snapped.

"But honest," Kiely quipped.

"Do you need anything before we leave?" Sadie asked, annoyance creasing her brow.

Kiely shook her head. "It's all good. I think we'll be fine. I'll get a message to you if I do."

"You really do look good with that baby," Pippa

said. "You look happy. Even relaxed and every time you look at his father your face lights up."

"Shut up, Pip!" Kiely snapped.

Her sisters laughed.

Kiely moved toward the entrance, Alfie in her arms and sound asleep against her shoulder. "I need to go lay him down," she said. "He's getting heavy."

"We're going to head back," Sadie said.

"Don't hurry off," Kiely said, just as Cooper came out the door.

"Are you two leaving?" he questioned. "Don't rush off."

Sadie nodded. "Yeah! We need to get back." She gave him a wave.

"If you let anything happen to our sister, we will come for you," Pippa said. She was pointing a finger at Cooper. "Trust and believe, we will come for you."

Cooper nodded. "I promise, I'll take good care of her."

"You better," Pippa admonished.

Kiely laughed. "Go away, Pip, and leave Cooper alone."

Pippa pressed her cheek to Kiely's. She trailed her hand against Alfie's back. "Be safe," she whispered, "and make sure he wears a condom!" Then she turned, her expression smug, leaving Kiely and Cooper standing side by side.

Kiely giggled, appreciating that for once, Pippa had gotten the last dig.

They watched as Sadie pulled the car back down the length of driveway and when they could no longer see the Suburban's rear lights, they turned to go into the house.

Claire had made arrangements for everything they could possibly need. A crib had been placed in the bedroom directly across from the master, an assortment of toys filling one corner. Kiely laid Alfie down and covered him with a newly purchased blanket. He stirred as if he might wake and then rolled into fetal position, continuing to slumber peacefully.

After a quick, self-guided tour of the house and the fully stocked refrigerator and cupboard, Kiely dropped down onto the sectional sofa and pulled a quilt around her torso. After everything that had happened she was feeling slightly squirrelly. The magnitude of how bad things could have been had suddenly hit. It had her feeling vulnerable and uneasy, fear and frustration not sitting well with her spirit.

Cooper came up from the basement. "Everything's good. We can communicate over the secure server so you can stay in touch with your family." He stopped short. The expression on her face made him pause. "Kiely? Are you okay?"

She shook her head, waving a dismissive hand. Tears formed and she struggled not to let them fall. Closing her eyes, she took a deep breath and held it, counting from one to ten in her head. She felt her bottom lip quiver ever so slightly. Minutes passed before she spoke.

"Does that fireplace work?" Kiely asked, gesturing with her head toward the stone structure that took up half a wall.

"I'm sure with enough firewood and a match we can get her working. I'll get right on that," he said.

Minutes later a fire was roaring in the fireplace. Flames crackled in vibrant shades of red, orange and yellow. Kiely pulled her knees to her chest, wrapping her arms around her legs. Cooper dropped down onto the sectional, sliding up beside her. She lifted the blanket to share the covering and he eased gently against her, extending his legs out in front of him.

"Do you want to talk about it?" he asked, cutting a quick eye in her direction.

"It hit me that we could have been killed tonight. Thinking about it has me rethinking my entire life. The risks I take. The choices I sometimes make to get a job done. What I want going forward. What changes I may need to make. It's just a whole lot. There's so much going through my head right now I'm finding it a little overwhelming."

\* \* \*

Cooper sighed. He understood because he too had been lost in his head about what had happened. He also knew that he didn't have the answers to make things better for either of them. Reaching for her hand, he entwined her fingers with his own. Kiely leaned her head back against his shoulder and he leaned his head against hers.

The crackling of the fire, a clock that ticked loudly, and a slow drip from the kitchen faucet were the only sounds through the room. The warmth from the fire wafted through the space but there was the hint of a chill in the air. Comfort came as they settled into the sound of each other breathing.

The morning sunrise found them both sleeping soundly, still sitting side by side. Cooper cradled her body with his own, his arms wrapped protectively around her. The fire had died down hours earlier and they were snuggled close together beneath the quilted blanket they shared. It was bliss that he knew he would not soon forget.

# Chapter 8

Adjusting to their new surroundings was proving to be more of a challenge than either of them had anticipated. Alfie was temperamental and whiney from the moment he woke. Clearly, he was not having a good day. So maybe she wasn't the kid whisperer she'd dubbed herself, she thought as Alfie threw his third, or maybe fourth, tantrum of the day and it wasn't yet noon.

She stood with both hands on her hips as the little boy threw himself to the floor kicking and screaming. This time he'd wanted chocolates that he'd seen in a jar in the pantry. One hadn't been enough and now he wasn't at all happy with Kiely telling him he couldn't have any more. Kiely watched him like he was an alien creature let loose in the middle of the room.

Cooper laughed. "And you said he was an angel!"

"I think he's possessed," she said.

"Just ignore him. He'll tire himself out in a while."

Kiely shook her head. "I don't want him to hurt himself."

"He won't. Trust me. That kid knows exactly what he's doing. Right now he's playing on your feelings. Hoping you'll let him have that candy."

"Well, we're not going to do that. It's lunchtime anyway," she said as she stepped over the child and moved to the kitchen.

Alfie revved his screaming up a notch.

"Do you need help?" Cooper asked, moving into the kitchen with her.

She shook her head. "No. Thank you for offering though. We're having handmade pizza. There's a baking stone!" she said, a hint of excitement in her voice. She punched down the dough she'd made shortly after their pancake breakfast.

"I think I've gained ten pounds since you arrived."

Kiely laughed. "Well, it looks good on you."

Cooper gave her a warm smile. "I'm going to take the munchkin for a walk. Hopefully he'll be in a better mood when we get back. Once he goes down for his nap we need to get some work done."

Kiely watched as Cooper scooped Alfie up off the floor and into his jacket, mittens and boots. He'd finally stopped screaming but the look he gave Kiely said he wasn't quite ready to be her friend again anytime soon. As father and son headed out the door she blew a sigh of relief and savored the moment of quiet. She punched the pizza dough a second time.

Cooking calmed her and Kiely planned to cook until she felt like herself again. Lunch was personal pizzas topped with Swiss chard, sausage and fresh mozzarella. She thought about baking cookies to make amends to Alfie. Moving to the pantry she found enough ingredients to make a few chocolate chip treats.

An hour later the smells of chocolate and vanilla filled the space. When Cooper and Alfie came back through the door both paused in the doorway, taking deep breaths to inhale the scent.

Cooper hummed. "Mmm! Something smells good in here."

Alfie peeled out of his coat and came running to her. "Ki-Ki!"

Kiely leaned down to give him a hug.

"I sorry Ki-Ki. Me was a bad boy. Alfie will be good, okay?"

She hugged him a second time. "Thank you, Alfie."

"I lub you, Ki-Ki!" he exclaimed as he threw his arms around her neck and kissed her cheek.

Kiely blinked away a tear. "I love you, too, Alfie."

"I hungry, Ki-Ki!"

"You take Daddy and help him wash his hands and then you two come back to get lunch. Okay?"

Alfie nodded. "Wash you hands, Dad-dy! Wash you hands!" He turned and raced toward the bathroom.

"He and I had a very long conversation about that tantrum," Cooper said. He tapped Kiely's arm, the gesture kind and tender.

"Go wash your hands," she muttered as she swiped a tear away. "Before you both have me crying!"

Cooper grabbed two more cookies and a glass of milk. Although he was stuffed from lunch, he just couldn't help himself. They were that good and Alfie had finally gone to sleep so that he could enjoy the dessert without having to share. He moved to the sofa, taking the seat across from Kiely.

"I made those for Alfie," she said. "I didn't want him to stay mad at me over that candy issue."

"I left him some."

"I'm going to have to send my sister a grocery list so I can make some more."

"People in protective custody don't usually cook gourmet meals."

"I'm treating this little adventure as a spa holiday of sorts."

Cooper smiled. "A working holiday, I hope. I could really use your help figuring out who this woman is. I'm coming up with blanks. Nothing makes any sense."

"Don't feel bad. I've been thinking about her all morning, too. I've eliminated more women from the suspect pool than I've been able to consider." Kiely sighed.

"I keep thinking about Abigail Matthews. You said you don't think she's involved, but do you think she might know something? Something that might make sense to us even if it doesn't make sense to her?"

"She doesn't, but maybe she'll remember something if we ask again. I doubt it but it won't hurt."

"Since you know her, I'm going to ask you to give her a call. She might be more inclined to open up and speak with you than with me. Meanwhile I'm going to see if forensics came up with anything from the explosion."

"Yes, sir," Kiely said as she gave him a salute.

Cooper shook his head, swallowing his last bite of cookie. "Beautiful and funny!"

"Damn right!" Kiely said as she rose from the table. "And it's a lethal combination."

Kiely reached out to Griffin before calling Abigail. It had taken her sisters less than twenty-four hours to fill their brothers in on what she'd been doing and all that had happened and now they wanted answers she wasn't yet interested in giving.

"So, Riley says this Cooper guy is good people. But he has a kid. Are you ready to do kids, Kiely? That's an important step, and I speak from experience," he said reminding her of what he and Abigail had gone through to adopt their foster child Maya.

"We're just friends, Griffin."

"That's not what Pippa said."

"Can I just talk to Abigail, please?"

"Don't change the subject, Kiely."

"I'm not. I'm trying to work and you want to discuss my personal life. And you know that is off limits."

"Maybe to strangers, not to family, right?" There was a hint of sarcasm in his tone that Kiely picked up on but ignored. Griffin sighed. "She should be home if you're planning to call her now. I just had lunch with her and Maya, and the baby was going down for a nap."

"I need to make time to come by and see my new niece. I promise to do that soon."

"Yes, you do and I'm going to hold you to that."

"Love you!"

"Stay safe, Kiely!"

Disconnecting the call, Kiely sat back in her chair, thinking about her big brother. Griffin had been adopted when he'd been eight years old and she'd been six. He'd been a foster kid first and much like Brody, their father had seen his potential, believing in him even when he was unsure. Both their parents had loved him like he was their own. But there had always been something holding Griffin back from feeling like he belonged…until recently. Like he was really a Colton and not just carrying the name by default. Since he'd met Abigail and Maya, he'd changed and opened up more.

Any time Griffin mentioned family he always sounded like he needed a pep talk. That he needed to be reminded that they loved him immensely and considered him kin, whether they were related by blood or not. But right then she didn't have time to coddle his feelings and sing him a rendition of "Kumbaya." It would have to wait until she saw him next in person. She engaged the secure phone line and dialed Abigail's number.

Abigail answered on the third ring. "Hello?"

"Abigail, hello! It's Kiely."

"Kiely, hey! How are you?"

"I'm well. Is this a good time to talk?"

"Can you hold on for a second? Just let me check on Maya. She's teething and it takes forever for her to fall asleep lately."

"That's not a problem at all." Kiely waited, listening to the silence on the other end.

Abigail came back to the phone quickly. "Sorry

about that. She's out like a light! What can I do for you?"

"I had some questions about your father."

Abigail groaned. "You know he and I don't have a relationship, right? It's been a while since I last spoke with him."

"I do. But we're trying to identify a woman who's connected to him. Someone he may be close to. She would be very protective of him. A girlfriend or lover, maybe?"

"Wes really isn't the relationship type."

"Maybe the two had a short-term fling?"

"I don't know."

"This woman has more of an athletic frame and she rides a motorcycle."

Abigail paused, seeming to think about who might fit that description. "I'm sorry, Kiely," she finally said. "I don't ever remember seeing him with someone like that."

"When was the last time you saw your father?"

"It's been a few months. My birthday actually, so it was in June. He dropped off a birthday gift."

"Do you remember what you talked about?"

"Actually, I do. He said that he'd gotten a new investor that he was very excited about. In fact, he made a crude comment about her becoming my new stepmother if she dropped a few pounds! He was so infuriating! I started screaming at him and told him what a horrible person I thought he was and how much I hated him. He was genuinely perplexed, like he couldn't understand what the problem was. He left after that and I haven't seen him since."

"Do you know who the investor was that he was referring to?"

"Sorry, Kiely. Since I never heard anything about a marriage or an engagement I never gave it another thought. I figured he was just talking out the side of his neck or maybe this mystery woman hadn't lost those extra pounds," she said sarcastically.

Kiely could hear the disgust in Abigail's voice and scathing tone. She could also detect the hurt and frustration. Knowing Abigail and Wes had not had a relationship for years, Kiely thought of her own father and the abundance of love that he had showered down on her and her siblings. Kiely had been a daddy's girl, her father the first man she trusted. She couldn't begin to fathom what it had to be like for Abigail to have a father like Wes Matthews. The young woman had gone through a lot when people discovered the connection between the two. She'd been bullied, threatened, and attacked, despite discovering the ricin connection to Revita-You and sounding the appropriate alarms. Others hadn't trusted her and wanted her to pay for her father's crimes, considering her guilty by virtue of her bloodline.

Recently, Abigail had been framed for a murder she didn't commit. Despite being completely exonerated, she had found that the allegations had threatened her custody and pending adoption of Maya. Griffin had come to her rescue, riding in like a knight on a white horse. His actions had solidified the bond between them. Watching their happily ever after unfold had been the stuff of romance novels.

"Abigail, I really appreciate you taking time to speak with me. You've been a big help."

"I haven't. Not really. I wish I could tell you more. I really want you to catch him."

"We will. Don't you worry. Drinks are on me the next time I see you!"

The baby suddenly cried in the background.

"And that would be Maya calling for my attention. I have to run."

"I understand. Talk to you soon," Kiely said as Abigail disconnected the call.

Kiely sat for a moment thinking about what Abigail had told her. She replayed the details of the case over in her head. The initial investigation into RevitaYou had found investors personally recruited by Wes Matthews. Those three had recouped their investment and then some, actually doubling their money. The investors that followed hadn't been so lucky.

It had been a typical pyramid scheme where money collected from newer victims was used to pay earlier victims, providing a veneer of legitimacy. All the victims were induced to recruit others, Wes

Matthews promising them recruitment commissions for their efforts. It was fraud, plain and simple. By the time Brody had invested, it was too late. Soon after it was discovered that RevitaYou was actually killing patients. Landon Street, the chemist behind RevitaYou had disappeared and so had Wes Matthews, with close to a million dollars of other people's money. Now someone close to Matthews didn't want law enforcement to find him.

Why? Was it personal? What was her motive? Was she a lover wanting to be a ride or die for her man? Or was her motive about revenge? Was she a lover scorned who wanted to find him herself without interference? And what was her connection to Cooper? Why had she singled him out to torment? None of it made an ounce of sense and there were still too many pieces missing from the puzzle.

Kiely moved down the hall to peek in on Alfie. He was still sleeping soundly and she imagined his lengthy walk had worn his little body out. She also knew he'd be wide open when he did wake, needing lots of attention.

She headed down the carpeted steps to the lower level where Cooper was working on his laptop. He wore a black T-shirt that clearly defined his muscles. He really was quite a handsome man. He was staring intently, reading something on the computer screen and there was something about this that was very attractive. She almost hated interrupting him. Almost. "Are you busy?"

Cooper looked up and smiled at her. He shook his head. "Just reading my emails. What's up?"

Kiely moved to the chair beside him and sat down. "I just spoke to Abigail about her father."

"Was she able to give you anything?"

"Not really, but she did mention an investor Wes may have been involved with romantically. Do you have a list of those women who gave him money?"

"I do." Cooper pulled a manila folder from the corner of the desk and began fumbling through the large stack of papers inside. "Here we are," he said as he found what he was looking for. "There were three initially who made out well. Jane Rodriguez, Marley Runyon and Meghan Otis. And a few others after who all lost their money."

"What do you know about them?"

"These three were the first investors. Their stories were instrumental in helping to secure the other investors. They got their money back plus sizeable profits for their efforts. All three also appear on RevitaYou promotional material."

"Have you talked with any one of them?"

"Not personally. I believe other agents with our fraud and cybercrimes divisions did." He punched keys on his keyboard, then nodded. "Agent Jeff Taylor spoke with all three and filed his report at

# Get Up To 4 Free Books!

Dear Reader,

***IT'S A FACT:*** if you answer 4 quick questions, we'll send you 4 FREE REWARDS from each series you try!

Try **Harlequin® Romantic Suspense** books featuring heart-racing page-turners with unexpected plot twists and irresistible chemistry that will keep you guessing to the very end.

Try **Harlequin Intrigue® Larger-Print** books featuring action-packed stories that will keep you on the edge of your seat. Solve the crime and deliver justice at all costs.

## Or **TRY BOTH!**

I'm not kidding you. As a leading publisher of women's fiction, we value your opinions... and your time. That's why we are prepared to reward you handsomely for completing our mini-survey. In fact, we have 4 Free Rewards for you, including 2 free books and 2 free gifts from each series you try!

Thank you for participating in our survey,

*Pam Powers*

# To get your 4 FREE REWARDS:
## Complete the survey below and return the insert today to receive up to 4 FREE BOOKS and FREE GIFTS guaranteed!

## "4 for 4" MINI-SURVEY

**1** Is reading one of your favorite hobbies?

  ☐ YES      ☐ NO

**2** Do you prefer to read instead of watch TV?

  ☐ YES      ☐ NO

**3** Do you read newspapers and magazines?

  ☐ YES      ☐ NO

**4** Do you enjoy trying new book series with FREE BOOKS?

  ☐ YES      ☐ NO

Please send me my Free Rewards, consisting of **2 Free Books from each series I select** and **Free Mystery Gifts**. I understand that I am under no obligation to buy anything, as explained on the back of this card.

❑ **Harlequin® Romantic Suspense** (240/340 HDL GQ5A)
❑ **Harlequin Intrigue® Larger-Print** (199/399 HDL GQ5A)
❑ **Try Both** (240/340 & 199/399 HDL GQ5M)

FIRST NAME        LAST NAME

ADDRESS

APT.#      CITY

STATE/PROV.      ZIP/POSTAL CODE

EMAIL ❑   Please check this box if you would like to receive newsletters and promotional emails from Harlequin Enterprises ULC and its affiliates. You can unsubscribe anytime.

HI/HRS-520-MS20

the beginning of the investigation. Obviously, they didn't have any complaints. They made money on their deals."

"Can we look at all the female investors? I know of one, Ms. Blythe Kent. My brother Riley is engaged to her niece, Charlize. Ms. Kent invested almost fifty grand and lost it all. She's up there in age, though, so I know she's not hot rodding around on a motorcycle. I'd also like to figure out who Matthews might have been involved with besides Landon Street."

"You think that's who might be our kidnapper?"

"It might be a long shot but it's all we have right now. I just know whoever doesn't want him found has to be personally connected to him."

Cooper typed again. "Jane Rodriguez…she doubled her initial investment. She's sixty years old and a retired teacher." He turned the computer screen so Kiely could see her picture.

"I don't think it's her," she said. "She looks like someone's grandmother."

Cooper shook his head and typed again. "Marley Runyon also doubled her initial investment. She is newly married and very pregnant. I'd say by this recent social media post that she's close to eight months along."

"The woman on the motorcycle was definitely not pregnant."

"And lastly, we have Meghan Otis." Cooper paused, reading the screen.

"What?" Kiely asked. She shifted forward in her seat.

"Meghan Otis, thirty-five years old, former college track star. Worked as a bank teller and won one hundred and fifty thousand dollars in the lottery six months ago. According to this she was instrumental in helping bring investors to RevitaYou and reportedly, she personally used the product."

"Any pictures?"

Cooper grinned. "Yes, check this out."

Meghan Otis was quite the selfie queen. There were hundreds of pictures of her on her social media accounts. Meghan working out. Meghan eating. Meghan hanging with friends. And a favorite for Kiely and Cooper, a picture of Meghan with her arms draped around Wes Matthews's neck.

"So did Matthews prey on Meghan because she had money?" Kiely questioned.

"That's highly probable. I wouldn't put anything past Matthews."

"But what was in it for her? It looks like she had everything going for her. Smart, accomplished, financially independent. And she's pretty! Why would she even consider using RevitaYou? It wasn't like she needed it."

Cooper shrugged. "Who knows why women do

what they do. I stopped trying to figure you and your kind out years ago."

Kiely laughed. "My kind? You have some nerve!"

Cooper shrugged a second time, pushing his broad shoulders toward the ceiling. "I'll put in a request for everything we can find about Meghan Otis."

"I'd like to go talk to her, too."

"Let's get the background information back first, and then we can figure that out."

Kiely looked down at her wristwatch. "Should we wake up Alfie? He's been asleep for almost two hours now."

"Give him a few more minutes. He did a lot of running when I took him for a walk."

"I just don't want him to be wide awake tonight because he slept so long this afternoon."

"I agree, but I don't think we'll have a problem."

An awkward silence danced between them, as she consciously tried to pretend that she wasn't feeling the rise of sexual tension that existed when they were in each other's presence. Kiely watched his mouth, thinking that kissing him would be the greatest joy. Both sat with clenched fists, struggling not to touch the other and desperate to shake away the fantasies that were coming all too frequently.

Kiely stood up abruptly. "I'm going to head back upstairs."

Cooper nodded. "I need to finish up some paper-work here. Then I need to call and see where we are with your friend Gunther."

"Not a problem. As soon as Alfie wakes up and has his snack, he and I are going to go outside to play in the leaves." Kiely was already at the bottom of the stairs. She gave him a wave and disappeared to the upper level of the home.

Cooper was smiling, and he felt slightly foolish. He found himself fighting not to gush when he and Kiely were in a room together. She had a way of amusing him even when he was trying to be seri-ous. There was something very special about Kiely Colton. She was sunshine in the midst of a storm. Her carefree spirit was like a breath of fresh air. She was light in a well of darkness. She was everything he had been missing in his life. He had vowed to never love again, but something about Kiely had him reconsidering that pledge. Something about her had him rethinking what love might look like in his future.

He appreciated her kindness toward his son. She was exceptionally good with the little boy and Alfie adored her. Alfie, who was usually shy around other people, most especially women, had told Kiely that he had "lub" for her. His childlike admission had been sweet and joy-filled. Cooper suddenly wished he had the courage and wisdom of a two-year-old, so that he could tell Kiely he was falling in love with her, too.

Because what he was suddenly feeling for Kiely Colton felt very much like love. It was energizing and nourishing and made him want to be a better man. It left him happy and excited by the prospect of each new day. It was desire and passion and longing like he couldn't ever remember feeling. It had him feeling blessed.

Cooper rose from his seat and shook out his arms and legs, anxious to shake away the tension that had spread through his body. He sat back down and reached for the phone. He'd missed a call from Lieutenant McKellar, who had left a message for him to call back as soon as he was able. When he didn't answer, Cooper left him a message.

He sat for a moment weighing his options; trying to determine what it was he needed and wanted to do. Reaching for his phone a second time, he dialed the district attorney's office. His secretary was all too happy to tell him that Eugene Beckwith was gone for the day. Leaving a second message for the man, Cooper wished her a good day and disconnected the line.

Cooper suddenly looked down to the notepad he'd been doodling on. A line of little hearts decorated the page, Kiely's name and his block printed in the center. Feeling foolish again, Cooper shook his head. He was grateful Kiely hadn't witnessed his adolescent behavior. Then again, he thought, maybe it was exactly what he needed to break the ice and open the conversation about what he was feeling. Tearing the top sheet of paper from the pad, he folded it in half and slid it into the back pocket of his jeans.

# Chapter 9

Kiely stood in the spray of hot water, allowing it to rain down over her shoulders. It trickled over her breasts and puddled beneath her feet. The body wash smelled of Japanese cherry blossoms, the delicate scent one of her favorites. She lathered herself from head to toe and then stood beneath the water to rinse it away. She was grateful for the moment, enjoying the quiet.

It had been a busy afternoon. Alfie had been on overload times ten. From the moment he'd woken from his nap, he had called her name over, and over again. Ki-Ki! Ki-Ki! Ki-Ki! It had sounded like a mantra for preschoolers. Being able to take the child outside to run and play had been a godsend. His energy was abundant and Kiely joked that if she could find a way to bottle and sell it, it would make them millions. Cooper had joined them and they had stomped through the woods, thrown leaves and hiked the trails behind the property. Alfie's laugh had been infectious and Kiely had had the best time.

Before they'd known it, it had been time for dinner. It had taken no time at all to toss the chicken she had marinated into the oven and to prepare a salad. Mashed garlic potatoes rounded out the meal. Both Cooper and Alfie had eaten heartily, the fresh air and outdoor activities triggering their appetites. Brownies topped with vanilla ice cream had been the perfect dessert. After his bath and thirty minutes of playing in the bubbles, Alfie had gone right to sleep. Once he was down for the night, Kiely had stolen a few minutes for herself, the hot shower feeling like heaven.

Her fingers and toes were shriveled when she finally stepped out of the glass enclosure and cut off the water. She felt like new money. Every muscle was relaxed and her skin was glowing. Her Japanese cherry blossom lotion was the last layer before a few spritzes of body spray. For ten minutes Kiely debated which pair of panties to wear and then she had to question why. This wasn't a date and she was acting like Cooper was taking her dining and dancing. Kiely was excited about spending time with him as if they hadn't just spent the entire day together. Feeling like a teen with her first crush, Kiely was struggling not to act like one.

Kiely dropped down against the corner of the bed, a heavy sigh blowing past her lips. There had been men in her life before Cooper. Men she had liked and men she was still friendly with. There were one or two who were friends with benefits, only calling on each other when there was no one else in their lives to satisfy those intimate urges. Calling on them when battery-powered Bob wasn't enough. But Kiely couldn't say that she had ever been in love with any man because she'd been fearful of failing herself the way she'd seen her parents fail each other. She didn't want to trust her heart and have her heart be disappointed. She didn't want to be her mother, putting a man first while losing herself in the process. Her life was simpler without a relationship and Kiely always chose simple when the opportunity presented itself. Men complicated things; her feelings, her time, her head. Men disrupted her flow and made her second-guess her own wants and dreams as she tried to navigate theirs. Keeping all men at arm's length, far from her heart, protected her.

But there was something about Cooper that had her letting her guard down. Something grounded and comfortable. Though she considered him a friend that something had her wanting more and imagining the possibilities had her completely dis-combobulated. Everything about their situation was foreign to her. Had anyone told her she'd be playing mommy and acting like a wife she would have told them they were lying. It surprised her how easily she had slid into the roles and how much she was enjoying them. Alfie had stolen her heart, but truth be told, so had his father.

Cooper was sitting on the sectional, playing with the television remote. A second helping of brownie and ice cream sat in a bowl on the coffee table. He'd also opened a bottle of wine and had poured them both a glass. He stopped to stare as she moved toward him, his eyes skating up and down the length of her body. Awe painted his expression and Kiely suddenly liked how she saw herself in his eyes.

She pointed at his bowl. "Really, Cooper?"

"It's all your fault. You're an amazing cook and you keep making these incredible desserts to tempt me. What else can I do?"

Kiely laughed. She moved to the kitchen. Her laugh faded quickly. "That was the last brownie! How many have you eaten?"

"Just grab another spoon. I'll share!"

"Yes, you will," she said as she pulled a utensil from the drawer and moved back to the sectional to sit with him. She swiped two bites of brownie before she scooted up to sit beside him. "So, any news on Gunther?"

"Your boyfriend Tripp and I are playing phone tag. I'll try him again in the morning."

"My boyfriend Tripp? You're funny!"

"I saw how he was looking at you."

"And how was that?"

"The way he's always winking his eye at you and that smirk on his face. I'm sure I don't have to explain it to you."

"No," she said, shaking her head, "you really do."

"I can't explain it. It was just inappropriate."

"You really are funny! That man is not interested in me and I am not interested in him."

"You sure about that?"

Kiely changed the subject abruptly. "The night the bombs went off you were about to say something to me."

Cooper paused and his cheeks suddenly flushed a bright shade of red. "Was I? I don't recall…"

"You recall," Kiely laughed.

"Has anyone told you that you can be slightly intimidating?"

"I intimidate you?"

"No! Not me! But I'm sure…well…" He suddenly stammered and then he laughed.

Kiely giggled with him. "I can't believe you're tongue-tied."

Cooper tossed up his hands. "You do that to me."

"Do what?"

"You know what."

"How long are we going to play this game?"

"As long as it takes for me not to make a complete and total fool out of myself. I don't know how to do this anymore." He suddenly looked exasperated.

Kiely shifted her body closer, settling into his body heat. She hooked her arm through his and leaned her head on his shoulder. "Tell me what it was you were going to say before that madwoman on the motorcycle interrupted us."

Cooper sighed, a soft breath of air blowing past his lips. "Before we were so rudely blown out of the moment, I was trying to tell you how I was feeling."

"And how were you feeling?" Kiely asked.

Cooper hesitated, trying to choose his words carefully. He cut his eye at her, holding his breath deep in his lungs. He suddenly felt completely out of his depth and he knew it showed.

Kiely spun her body around to face him, sitting with her legs crossed lotus style. "You like me, don't you?" She met his stare, a hint of mischief shimmering in her eyes.

Her expression made him smile. "Yeah, I do. I like you a lot."

She tapped his leg gently with her hand. "I like you, too, Cooper."

His smile pulled into a full grin. "You do?"

"Why does that surprise you?"

"Because I don't get the impression that there are too many people you actually like."

Kiely laughed. "So now you have jokes!"

Cooper laughed with her. He took another deep breath, his expression turning serious. "I know this whole situation with us has been awkward."

"It's been interesting. Maybe not ideal, but it's felt pretty darn special."

"That's one way to look at it."

Cooper reached for her hand and held it, studying her fingers. She had the hands of a piano player, he thought. Her fingers were long, her nails cut short and manicured with a light coat of pale pink polish.

"Are you interested in a relationship, Cooper?" Kiely was eyeing him intently. Watching him as he was watching her.

"After Sara died, I'd sworn off any kind of relationship. I'd pretty much given up on love. But yeah, since you and I have been getting to know each other, I'm very interested in seeing where we can go from here. But can I be honest with you?"

"I would hope you wouldn't have to ask. I expect honesty, Cooper. I don't ever want to be lied to."

He gave her a nod of his head. "This scares me, Kiely. I was never any good at dating. And I'm sure if she were here, my wife would tell you that I wasn't great at marriage either. I just don't want you to move forward thinking I have a clue about how to do this."

"Well, the way I figure it, we can stress over it or we can just make it up as we go along. And I don't stress out over anything," Kiely said softly.

"You really are an amazing woman, Kiely Colton."

"Yes, I am, and you'll have to work hard to earn me."

Cooper chuckled. "I just knew you were going to be high maintenance!"

The conversation was suddenly interrupted as Alfie came scampering across the room in their direction. Kiely's eyes widened as she tossed Cooper a look. "Alfie! Are you okay?"

"Want my Ki-Ki!" he exclaimed as he climbed onto the sectional and into Kiely's lap. "Where you go, Ki-Ki?"

Kiely hugged him. "Kiely's right here, sweetie. Why are you awake?"

"Did he climb out of the crib?" Cooper said, still looking stunned.

"You didn't know he could climb out?"

"You mean this wasn't his first time?"

She laughed, giving Alfie a tickle. "Your daddy is so silly!"

Alfie giggled. "Silly, Dad-dy!"

Cooper leaned forward to kiss his son's cheek.

And then he pressed his lips to Kiely's cheek, the kiss lingering until Alfie pushed him away.

"No kiss my Ki-Ki, Dad-dy. Dat *my* Ki-Ki!"

Cooper noticed he and Kiely were working well together, playing easily off each other's strengths and weaknesses. This dynamic give-and-take allowed them to discover more about each other as they continued to research the case. The friendship that had blossomed was full and thick. Their time together felt as natural as breathing and both found themselves wishing that it would never have to end. Conversation was sometimes intense and sometimes nonsensical. Laughter was abundant as they realized they were more alike than they were different.

When Cooper and Tripp finally connected, the call coming in the early evening two days later, Kiely excused herself from the room, heading back upstairs to check on Alfie. They exchanged smiles and Cooper winked his eye at her.

"Only my boyfriend does that," she said smugly as she pointed to the phone and the call that was on hold.

Cooper laughed. "I deserved that!"

"Yes, you did."

She waved her hand at him. "I'll be upstairs with the baby," she said, disappearing from his sight.

Cooper reached for the telephone receiver. "Tripp, hello! Sorry to keep you holding."

"It's not a problem. I'm glad we've finally caught up with each other. There's a lot I need to fill you in on. You want the good news or the bad news?"

"It's like that?"

"Why don't I just start with the good news. We've got a name!" Tripp said excitedly.

"Gunther came through?"

"Not before asking for a down pillow and cashmere blanket to go with everything else he wanted."

"That guy's a real piece of work."

"That he is. I just emailed you the report. According to him, the man behind Capital X is named Tate Greer."

Cooper frowned. Tate Greer? The name was familiar but he wasn't sure where he'd heard it before. "What do we know about him?"

"That's it, right now. He's been running under the radar for a while. He's got no rap sheet. Not even a parking ticket. He's squeaky clean. Almost too clean."

"Are we sure the name's not an alias?"

"We're not sure of anything at the moment, but from everything Gunther told us, he's bad news: racketeering, fraud, embezzlement, solicitation and possibly a murder or two. He personally ordered the assault on Brody Higgins and all the others. I sent you Gunther's signed statement. Once he started talking we couldn't get him to shut up. He was crooning like a stuck canary."

Cooper had scrolled through a lengthy list of email messages and was printing off the documents that Tripp had sent. "This is good news. Good work, Lieutenant."

"Couldn't have done it without you, Agent. I don't know what you said to him, but he's not interested in ever seeing you again." Tripp laughed.

"What's the bad news?"

Tripp sighed. "We've had another death. The coroner is attributing it to the ricin-laced RevitaYou product. The mayor is on a rampage. He wants Landon Street caught and caught yesterday."

"Damn," Cooper cussed. He suddenly felt like he was losing traction with the case. "I really need to get back to my office," he said. "I'm limited in what I can do remotely."

"I get it," Tripp said. "But when you do come back you're going to be able to hit the ground running. You'll be well rested, healed and ready to kick ass. Meanwhile just do what you can do. We'll keep you in the loop here and call on you when we need you."

"Thank you," Cooper said, suddenly feeling bad about the names he'd called the man in his head. He realized they might actually be good friends one day and when that day came, he looked forward to laughing with him about his assumptions about Tripp and Kiely. "I'd like to buy you a beer when we close this case."

"I'm going to hold you to that," Tripp said. He continued. "My office also sent you the forensics report from the bombing at your property. It was a nondescript pipe bomb. There was nothing about it that we could connect to anyone already in our database. But we're not giving up."

"I appreciate that." And Cooper did, but it wasn't lost on him that they were no closer to finding the woman who'd taken his son than when they'd started. Which meant Alfie was still at risk.

The two men agreed to talk again later in the week after Cooper was able to read through all the reports. After disconnecting the call, he sat back in his seat, his mind racing. There was information he still needed and he began making a list of orders for his team at the agency. Even though he couldn't be there, he knew how to delegate well.

Finding Wes Matthews and his cohort Landon Street was at the top of his to-do list. He added the unknown woman who'd kidnapped Alfie and bombed his car. And now there was Tate Greer. Something told him the three men were connected. He needed to figure out how. And his instincts were shouting that the woman who had taken his son was a lone wolf and not necessarily doing the bidding of any one man. So, what was her connection to him and why his son?

Alfie suddenly called him from the top of the stairs. "Dad-dy! Dad-dy!"

Cooper called back. "Yes, son? What's wrong, baby?"

"Me and Ki-Ki making cookies!" he exclaimed excitedly. The pitter-patter of his little feet running back to the kitchen echoed after him.

Cooper smiled. Alfie and Kiely were definitely a thing. He had high hopes that if all continued to go well, he and Kiely would be a thing, too.

Hours later Alfie was down for the night and he and Kiely were enjoying cups of hot chocolate laced with bourbon and the white chocolate cranberry cookies she and Alfie had made. This was quickly becoming his favorite time of day, when he and Kiely sat side by side, their conversation easy. Sometimes they talked and sometimes they didn't. This night Kiely was scrolling through her iPad reading recipes while he watched some Jimmy Kimmel special on the television.

"I had a good conversation with Tripp," Cooper said, when she finally laid the iPad down.

"That's good."

"The case is…"

"Let's not talk about the case. Not tonight. We've been working the case all day and I need to take a step back from it. Please."

Cooper met the look she was giving him with one of his own. He nodded. "That's fine."

"Did you take your meds?"

"No. I actually feel good. I haven't needed a pain pill all day."

"That's good. You may want to take one before you go to bed to ensure you rest well."

He shrugged. "Maybe."

"Wanna play a game?" Kiely questioned.

Cooper grinned. "A game?"

"Twenty questions. We ask each other ten questions and each has to be answered. No shirking off an answer because you don't like what was asked."

Cooper eyed her curiously. His gaze narrowed just a smidge. "Why does this feel like it's going to get me in trouble?"

"I guess that all depends on your answers," Kiely said with a warm laugh.

He sat upright. "Okay, I'm game to play."

"What's your favorite color?"

"My favorite color? My favorite color is green."

"Okay, your turn."

"What's your favorite color?"

"You can't ask the same question."

"Why not? I want to know the answer."

"I'm going to give you this one, but don't do it again. My favorite color is beige."

"That's a color?"

"Is that your next question?"

Cooper held his hands up as if he were surrendering. "Sorry about that. Your turn."

"Name three people, living or dead, that you'd like to have dinner with if you could."

Cooper paused, giving the question a moment of thought. "My mother, my grandmother and Midge."

"Who's Midge?"

"Midge was a rottweiler I had when I was a little boy. She was my best friend for many years. We did everything together."

"Midge isn't a person."

"You didn't know Midge," he said, giving her a look.

"Okay," Kiely giggled. "But why not Sara? Wouldn't you want to see her again?"

"My wife?" Cooper shrugged, his gaze shifting off into the distance as he pondered the question. He turned his eyes back to her as he spoke. "One dinner wouldn't be enough time to apologize to her for being a crappy husband. It wouldn't be fair to her." He dropped the subject, contrition cloaking his expression. "Your turn," he said. "Who was the first boy you ever kissed?"

Amusement crossed Kiely's face. "His name was Steven. I don't remember his last name. We were in the third grade and he kissed me one day on the playground."

"What did you do?"

"I told my brother Riley and Riley punched him in the face."

"Ouch!"

"It wasn't pretty," she responded. "Why did you become an FBI agent?"

"I've always wanted to be in law enforcement since I was a kid. I thought being an agent with the FBI would be like an American James Bond adventure. I saw myself going undercover, with high-tech weapons and always catching the bad guys. At the time it looked like a great career path."

"And now?"

"There are no cool weapons, rarely do I get to go in the field, undercover or otherwise, and it's been a great career path."

Kiely gave him a smile.

"French fries or hash browns?" Cooper questioned.

"French fries. Are you good at oral sex?"

Cooper choked on the swallow of hot chocolate he had just sipped. He was laughing and coughing at the same time, a blush of color warming his cheeks. "Really, Kiely?"

Her brow was raised as she looked at him. "Just answer the question."

He shook his head. "I've never had any complaints, but with all things, I'm sure practice will make perfect." Kiely gestured for him to ask his next question. "How long was your last relationship?"

"I've never really done relationships, but if you want to get technical about it, then the last guy I dated lasted ten days."

"Who broke it off, you or him?"

"I get the next question. It's not your turn."

"It was a two-part question. It should be allowed."

"Well, it's not."

Cooper laughed. "Fine! Ask your question."

"Do you like being a father?"

"I love being a father. It has made me a better man. And yes, I would love to have more children one day."

"I didn't ask that," Kiely said.

"But you were going to. That was clearly a two-part question."

"What are you doing, making up the rules as you go along?"

"I'm playing the game!"

Kiely folded her arms across her chest. "Ask your question."

"Your last relationship, who broke up with whom?"

"I broke up with him. There was no point staying when I knew it wasn't going to work out." Kiely shifted her body, stretching her arms outward. "Cats or dogs?"

"Definitely dogs. Cats jump on the counters in the kitchen when you're not home. I'm not a big fan of cats."

"That is not true!"

"How do you know? Do you have a cat?"

"I just know. And yes, I do. His name is Jim Morrison."

Cooper blinked. "Jim Morrison?"

Kiely laughed. "Ask your last question, Agent McKellar."

"My last? I didn't get ten questions, did I? You said I'd get ten questions."

"If I counted those two, you have exceeded your ten questions."

"You're one tough cookie, Kiely Colton!"

"You better ask before you lose your turn." She eyed him with a raised brow, waiting.

Curling his lips in an indulgent smile, Cooper grinned at her. He leaned forward in his seat, the gesture feeling very conspiratorial as Kiely leaned with him. "May I kiss you?" His voice came out in a husky whisper.

Kiely's expression shifted, her eyes widening. Her smile blossomed, light shimmering in her eyes. "A kiss?"

"Do I need to repeat the question?"

"No, I heard you."

Cooper repeated himself. "So then, can…I… kiss…you?" he repeated.

"Yes," Kiely finally answered. "I was wondering what was taking you so long to get to it!"

Shifting his body toward her, Cooper eased his

left arm around her waist and pulled her close. Kiely reached both arms around his neck as he leaned in against her. He brought his face near hers and then pulled back. He repeated the gesture a second time, coming so close that his warm breath blew gently against her lips. The third time his mouth connected with hers in the sweetest kiss Cooper had ever experienced. Her lips were like plush pillows, soft like satin and she tasted of chocolate and mint.

In that moment Cooper knew that he would never want to kiss any other woman ever again. He loved how Kiely melted into his arms and she felt like home. He would have sworn that he saw fireworks, flashes of light behind his eyes brilliantly celebrating the moment. His tongue tapped lightly against the line of her teeth waiting for her to allow him in. As their mouths danced beautifully together, Cooper felt like he'd reached the mystical harmonious valley of Shangri-La. Kiely's touch was sweeter than his favorite cookie, ice cream on a summer day, and the little nougat candies his mother would make for Christmas. In his arms, she was sunshine after a spring rain, the light at the end of a dark tunnel, and the answer to prayers he hadn't known he needed. That first kiss was everything and more.

## Chapter 10

Kiely was pleasantly exhausted the next morning. She and Cooper hadn't gone to bed until the wee hours of the morning. That first kiss had led to a second and then a third and before either knew it they were making out like teenagers in the back seat of his father's Ford automobile. The experience had been incredible.

Kissing Cooper had felt like a dream come true. His touch was gentle yet also commanding and slightly possessive. His hands had danced across her back and down the length of her torso with skillful precision. His heated fingertips had ignited currents of electricity through her body. He had taken her on a sensual journey of warm caresses and hot touches, the likes of which she had never experienced before. If she had to explain it to anyone she wouldn't have been able to find the words.

The moment had been interrupted when little Alfie had woken with a slight fever. It had taken a good hour to get him back to sleep and then they were both too exhausted to go back to making out. Alfie still wasn't feeling one hundred percent and had been moody most of the morning. While Cooper had gone downstairs to work, Kiely had rocked Alfie with a half-dozen storybooks, the child's song "Baby Shark" on constant rotation, and sips of apple ginger tea.

Alfie had finally gone down for a nap and Kiely was in the kitchen humming away when Cooper came back up the stairs.

She greeted him with a wide grin and an eye wink. "Hey, good-looking! What are you up to?"

"Something smells really good and I came to check out what you were into."

"I was just about to pull your lunch out of the oven. I made individual chicken pot pies."

Cooper tilted his head slightly, his look inquisitive. "Do I smell apples and cinnamon too?"

"That's tonight's dessert. Apple pie with a buttermilk and rosemary piecrust."

"Mmm!" Cooper hummed. "I can't wait! We'll have ice cream with that, right?"

Kiely laughed. "Does butter pecan work for you?"

"I swear I've gained at least twenty pounds since you came into my life. It's been the best twenty pounds I've ever had."

"As soon as the doctor gives you the all-clear we need to get you back in the gym. Are you a runner by chance?"

"I don't hate it, but it's not my favorite thing to do."

"Thank God!" Kiely exclaimed. "I despise running."

"What do you do to stay in shape?"

"Do I have to do something?"

Cooper laughed. "So, you want me to believe that you do nothing to maintain that great figure?"

"I was blessed with good genetics."

"I think I hate you. I really don't, but still!" He laughed.

"Come sit down and eat your lunch," Kiely commanded. "The pot pies are ready."

After plating the food, Kiely sat down at the table with him. The conversation was casual as they savored their lunch.

"I sent my sister a shopping list. She's going to come up tomorrow. Do you want her to bring you anything?" Kiely questioned.

Cooper suddenly sat forward. He dropped his fork against his plate. A light bulb had gone off in his head as a piece of the puzzle came together. "Your sister. What's her fiancé's name?" he asked.

Concern blessed Kiely's expression, the abrupt shift in Cooper's mood disconcerting. "Pippa? She's engaged to Emmanuel. Emmanuel Iglesias. Why?"

Cooper shook his head. "No, your sister, Sadie. Who's the boyfriend you and Pippa were giving her a hard time about on the ride up here?"

Kiely scowled. "Tate Greer. No one can stand him. He's a real creep."

"He's more than that," Cooper snapped as he suddenly stood and headed for the office downstairs. He called out over his shoulder. "Tate Greer is the mastermind behind Capital X. Gunther named him yesterday. The FBI has deemed him dangerous. He's been placed on our Most Wanted list."

For the briefest moment Kiely sat stunned. Her eyes had widened and heat flushed her face a deep shade of rising rage. Her mind began to race, her heartbeat on super speed. Fear was holding hands and doing a two-step with anger, the likes of which she hadn't felt in some time. She'd always known Tate Greer was scum. She never would have imagined that he was even lower, more like the fungus that fed on pond scum. She cussed, a lengthy stream of expletives blowing past her lips.

Dashing after him, Kiely followed Cooper downstairs, taking them two at a time. Her voice was an octave higher when she spoke. "I just talked with

Sadie about an hour ago. She wanted my recipe for fettuccine carbonara. She's meeting Tate at his condo tonight for dinner. They've been thinking about eloping to Vegas and she's supposed to give him her answer."

"We need to stop her," Cooper said. "She's not safe. Call your brother. I'm going to call Agent Miller."

Cooper and Kiely were both pacing the floor, anxiety levels at an all-time high. Alfie was still under the weather and Kiely held him close as she walked him back and forth. Her nervousness was doing very little to soothe the whining child's discomfort.

"It's going to be okay, Alfie. It's okay," she cooed.

The couple had spent the last few hours on the telephone, back and forth with Kiely's brother Riley and the FBI. Cooper had alerted his team and a plan was now in place to catch Tate Greer. The challenge for them, was being able to catch Tate and keep Sadie safe. Tipping him off could easily prove to be a detriment to her sister. And there was no way they could tell Sadie and trust that she wouldn't reveal their hand if her emotions got the best of her.

After much discussion it was decided to let Sadie proceed with her dinner plans. Shortly after six o'clock, Kiely would call her sister and say that she had an emergency. When Sadie exited the home to come to her aid there would be an FBI team waiting outside. Riley would also be there to ensure that Sadie was safe. When Sadie was out of harm's way the team could go in and apprehend Tate Greer. It sounded simple enough, but Kiely and Cooper both knew that anything could go wrong at any time.

Cooper was able to monitor his team's activity digitally, and the plan was that as soon as they were in place, Kiely would make the call. With the clock ticking Kiely's nerves were on overload. She hated that Sadie was in this position. Not following her instincts, and wanting her sister to be happy, Kiely hadn't vetted him as well as she should have. And she couldn't help but wonder if Tate's interest in Sadie had been purely selfish, if he'd been using her sister to keep a close eye on what was going on with the case. After reading the report on Tate, she knew that he was capable of anything. He wouldn't hesitate to use Sadie if it meant saving himself. And if he harmed her sister she didn't know what she would do.

"It's time," Cooper said, gesturing at her. He reached for Alfie, taking the child out of her arms. "Remember, it's okay if you let your anxiety show. Use it so that she knows you desperately need her."

Kiely gave him a nod as she moved to the desk to sit down. She had tried to not let him see her nervousness, but Cooper had picked up on it. She had no qualms about lying to her sister, but she didn't want to do anything that would put her family in harm's way. She took a deep breath then dialed her sister's number and waited for Sadie to answer.

"Hello?"

"Sadie, hey. It's me," Kiely responded.

"Hey, what's up? You calling to see if I executed the fettuccine correctly?"

"Are you alone or is Tate there with you?"

"He's in the shower, why? Are you okay, Kiely? You don't sound good."

"No, I really need your help. But you can't tell Tate."

"Does this have anything to do with Cooper and the kidnapping case?"

"Yes. I'm actually outside," Kiely said, the little white lie rolling easily off her tongue. "There's a black sedan parked across the street. Can you sneak out for a quick second and come see me? I can tell you everything then."

Kiely could almost see her sister moving to a front window to peer outside. She lied again, saying, "The FBI picked me up and brought me here. It's really important, Sadie! I really need to talk with you. But I don't want to involve Tate, so please don't tell him."

"Don't worry, he's still in the shower. I'll be right there. I'm on my way out."

"Thank you," Kiely said. For a split second she

wanted to apologize to her sister. To say she was sorry for the dishonesty. But more than anything she needed to know Sadie was safe from the likes of Tate Greer. She was desperate for her sister to know what kind of man he truly was but since she couldn't say those words, she said the next best thing. "I love you, Sadie."

Sadie disconnected the call and when she did, Kiely began to count. The few short minutes it took for her sister to exit the house and scurry across the street to the car felt like forever. When her eldest brother's number showed up on the phone, Kiely snatched it quickly.

"Hello?"

"We've got her. She's safe," Riley answered.

Kiely could hear her sister in the background, her voice raised as she questioned what was going on. Sadie fussing was all she needed to let go of the breath she'd been holding tightly in her lungs. When she exhaled, letting it go, warm breath and apprehension gushed from her like air from a popped balloon.

"She wants to talk to you," Riley said as Kiely listened to him passing their sister his phone.

"Kiely, what the hell is this?" Sadie snapped. "Where are you?"

"I'm still at the safe house with Cooper and Alfie. I'm sorry I had to lie to you. But Riley will explain everything."

"Somebody had better explain something to me!" Sadie shouted.

Riley had taken his phone back. "Tell Agent Winston I'll call him back with an update once everything goes down."

"Thanks, Riley! Love you, big brother!"

The phone line went dead. Kiely sat there for a moment, allowing herself to process it all. She couldn't begin to imagine what Sadie had to be feeling right then. Discovering that Tate Greer wasn't the man her sister thought he was would break her heart. Tate's deception would surely steal Sadie's joy. Understanding the magnitude of that left a bitter taste in Kiely's mouth.

As if he had a sixth sense, Cooper read her mood. "If you need to leave, I understand. I'm sure your sister needs you right now."

Kiely shook her head. "I need to be here with you and Alfie. Until we find that woman, neither one of you is safe. My family will make sure Sadie is okay. Besides, I'm sure I'm the last person she wants to see right now. She needs someone to blame and I'll be it while she figures it all out. I know her well."

Kiely rose from her seat. She moved swiftly to Cooper's side and into his arms. He hugged her tightly as she breathed a sigh of relief. She felt safe against him and could have held onto him forever.

She pressed her hand to Alfie's cheek. With Sadie secure under her brother's protective umbrella, keeping the little boy safe was now her first priority. Her family was everything to her and as far as she was concerned Alfie and his father were now family to her, too.

"He's still warm," she said. "It's time for another dose of baby medicine."

"Why don't you take him up and get him settled. I'll be up as soon as I hear something."

Kiely nodded, then reached to kiss his lips. She eased Alfie against her chest. "Come on, precious. Come to Kiely."

Hours later Alfie's fever had finally broken and he was sleeping comfortably. Kiely had tried to call her sister multiple times, but Sadie hadn't answered. Kiely had no doubt that Sadie was furious with her, needing someone other than Tate to blame. This too would pass, she thought. She thought about going back down to wait it out with Cooper, but he needed to focus and she needed a moment to herself.

When her phone rang, it surprised her. Recognizing Pippa's cell phone number, she answered it promptly.

"Hey, Pip!"

"Are you okay?" she asked.

Kiely felt her stomach flip. Since they'd been little girls they had always been oddly simpatico; one always knew when something was wrong with the other. Anytime Kiely was feeling blue, she trusted that Pippa would call like clockwork to check on her.

"I'm fine," Kiely answered.

"Don't lie, Kiely. I got that gut feeling that things were off with you."

Kiely sighed. "I'm just trying to work through some things. Have you spoken to Sadie?"

"She's here with me now. She's been bawling her eyes out since she got here."

"I hate that this has happened to her. But I'm glad that she knows the truth about Tate."

"We just need to make sure she knows we're here for her. She needs to feel supported and she'll get through it."

"I wish I was there."

"You just need to keep yourself safe. How are things with you and that handsome agent going?"

"Hold on," Kiely said. She moved down the hallway toward her bedroom to ensure Cooper couldn't overhear her conversation. She paused in the doorway to peek in on Alfie before disappearing behind her closed door and dropping down to the bedside.

"Don't laugh at me, Pippa, but I think I'm falling for Cooper."

Pippa laughed. "You think?"

"Okay, I know. I love him, and it scares me to death!"

"Why? That's such a beautiful thing!"

"Because I've become Mom! It's the craziest

thing, Pip, but all I want to do is take care of Cooper and Alfie. I feel like I've been transported back in time and discovered my inner June Cleaver," she said. "I don't even recognize myself anymore!"

"But are you happy?"

"Happier than I think I've ever been. But I'm sure Mom was happy, too, until she wasn't. I don't want to look back twenty years from now and regret that I gave up being a wild child for a man."

"Kiely, you've spent the majority of your adult life running toward danger in order to run from commitment to anything. Nothing has ever brought you true joy so that you would want to settle down and avoid always putting yourself at risk. This man and his son are bringing you joy. Embrace that! None of us knows what the future holds and change happens every day. Twenty years from now you may still be happier than you have ever been."

Kiely reflected on her sister's comment. "He kissed me," she said.

"Just kissed you?"

"We've been taking things slow."

"I'm thinking if you haven't been to bed with him already then this man is definitely the one."

"Why would you say that?"

"Because you have never had any qualms about sleeping with a man you were attracted to. Your hit-it and quit-it attitude has always concerned us. Because you've dated some really good guys, Kiely. Good guys that you tossed away like trash."

Kiely sighed.

The knock on the door pulled her from the reflections.

"Kiely?" Cooper called her name. She could hear the concern in his voice and it tugged at her heartstrings.

"I need to run," she said to Pippa. "Cooper is calling me. I'll check on Sadie tomorrow."

"Sadie will be fine. Vikki is on her way, and we'll take care of her. I may not come up there tomorrow as I planned. Will you be okay if I don't?"

"I'll be fine. Just take care of Sadie. Tell her I love her, please."

"We love you, too! And, please don't sabotage yourself trying to overthink this! Care for this man and know that it's okay if he feels the same."

Kiely stood up from the bedside and moved to the door, pulling it open. Cooper looked anxious, standing on the other side.

"Is everything okay?" he asked.

"I was just on the phone with Pippa. I wanted to check on Sadie. She's not answering any of my calls."

"I'm sorry."

"There's nothing for you to be sorry about. So, what's going on? Did your team complete their mission?"

Cooper shook his head, his expression dropping. "We lost him," he said.

"Lost him?" Her expression was incredulous, her eyes wide as saucers. "How the hell did they lose him?"

"We're still trying to figure that one out. They raided the townhouse and he wasn't there. The shower was still running but Tate was long gone. We're thinking he slipped out the back and managed to get past our men who were positioned there."

"Did Sadie say something to him before she left the house?"

"Not a word. Your brother says she was as surprised as they were."

"So that means he's on the run now, too." Kiely threw up her hands in frustration.

"It also means that Sadie might be in danger. Your brother has asked us to move her into protective custody."

"Well, she can come here and stay with us, right?"

"I already suggested that option, but Sadie refused. She says she just wants to be alone."

Tears misted Kiely's eyes and she batted her lashes so as not to cry. "She's devastated."

"Agent Miller will take her to another location first thing in the morning."

Kiely shook her head. "I can't believe this is happening," she said.

"There's more. I need to go back to Grand Rapids in the morning. I have a meeting with the mayor scheduled first thing and he wants to do a press conference."

"A press conference? Do you think that's wise?"

"I'll be fine and I won't do anything that will jeopardize you or Alfie's safety. But he's on a real tangent about us finding Landon Street and making sure the public is aware of the dangers of RevitaYou. Will you and Alfie be okay by yourselves for a few hours?"

"He and I will be just fine. I don't want you worrying about us."

Cooper pulled her into a deep hug and held on tightly. He kissed her forehead, his lips brushing gently against her skin. "I can't help but worry, Kiely. You two are the most important people in my life right now."

Cooper wasn't sure what to think. He was still fuming about that raid going bad; thinking that if he had been there on-site they would've captured Tate Greer. He hadn't planned to go back to Grand Rapids, but political pressure was bearing down on the FBI. What he hadn't told Kiely was that he also planned to participate in a second raid while he was in the city. A random tip had come in on the hotline with an address where the caller claimed Landon Street could be found. Landon Street's picture had been in the news for days. The Grand Rapids Police Department had even issued a reward for information about his whereabouts. A special line had been dedicated to accept the flood of calls that had followed.

Earlier in the investigation Cooper had spoken with Landon's half brother, Flynn Cruz-Street. With two tours of duty under his belt, Flynn now worked as military police at the Fort Rapids military base. In their brief conversation it was obvious that Flynn had once idolized his big brother. He had claimed they were now estranged, claiming not to know where Landon was but that he had since seen him twice around the city. Flynn had assured them that he would call if he spotted his sibling again and so far he had been true to his word. Flynn sounded anxious to find Landon himself, hoping to convince his brother to turn himself in. Despite Flynn's many assurances that he wanted to do what was right, Cooper wasn't sure that he truly trusted the man.

He needed to vet this new tip personally. He also knew that if he told Kiely, it would be an issue. She either wouldn't want him to go or she'd insist on going with him. Keeping her safe was now as important as keeping Alfie safe. He figured he would deal with the fallout after things were all said and done.

The rest of their evening had been relatively quiet. Kiely hadn't talked much, retiring to her bedroom early. Now he was missing her something crazy. After a hot shower he moved from the bathroom to the bedroom and climbed into his bed. He had checked on Alfie before his shower and his son seemed to be past the virus that had raised his temperature and put him in a sour mood. Cooper knew that his little boy would sleep soundly through the night.

He tossed and turned for another hour, unable to fall off to sleep. Cooper couldn't stop thinking about Kiely. There had been a sadness in her eyes, her sister's heartbreak fracturing her own. Knowing the siblings were close, it wasn't until he saw how hurt she was that he realized just how close.

Cooper would've done anything to take Kiely's pain from her. He couldn't begin to know how to console her. He just knew that he wanted to put a smile back on her face and make things well. Breaking this case would bring comfort to her and so many others.

The knock at his door surprised him. When Kiely pushed it open, easing into the room, that surprised him more. She wore a black tank top and matching panties. She'd pinned her hair up and a wisp of curls framed her face. Her skin was bare of makeup and her cheeks glowed. She was stunning. Stepping into the room Kiely turned to close and lock the door behind her. She moved to the nightstand and turned on the baby monitor.

"We need to hear Alfie in case he wakes up," she said softly.

Cooper nodded his agreement. Nervous energy exploded through his lower extremities. He suddenly wanted her more than he could have ever imagined. Throwing back the covers he gestured for her to climb in beside him. Kiely sat down on the mattress, lifted her legs and slid her body against his, her buttocks grazing his pelvis. As he covered them both with the blanket he wrapped his arms tightly around her, curling himself against her backside.

They lay together for a good while, trading easy caresses. Cooper pressed a damp kiss against Kiely's neck. Others followed, trailing over her shoulder. His touch was featherlight and he felt Kiely's entire body tremble. She grabbed his hand and pressed it to her breasts, which fit perfectly in the palms of his hands. Her nipples were rock-hard and as he gently kneaded the soft flesh Kiely slowly rotated her buttocks against the sizeable bulge that had risen in his flannel pants. The two did a sensual dance, lying side by side, cradled sweetly against each other.

When Kiely turned in his arms, pressing her mouth to his, that kiss felt as mesmerizing as their first kiss. Her tongue did a voracious tango in his mouth, teasing past the line of his teeth to dance with his tongue. Her warm breath was minty, tasting like the mouthwash they both used. Kiely's hands skated against his chest, wound around his back and settled along the round of his backside.

His heart fluttered and blood surged through every vessel in his body. His muscles tightened and when she slid her hand past his waistband, wrapping her fingers around his male member, Cooper thought he would explode right then and there. Their loving became feverish, heat rising like a vengeance between them. They tore at each other's clothing, desperate to feel skin against skin.

Cooper pulled himself from her just long enough to reach a condom hidden in his wallet resting on the nightstand. He sheathed himself quickly. When he rolled above her, Kiely parted her legs widely and welcomed him in. That moment of intimate connection, as Cooper slid his body into hers, affirmed what both had been feeling. Love spiraled in brilliant shades of joy and delight. It was thick and abundant and all-consuming. The pleasure was one he never would have fathomed. It was sensual gratification and hedonistic decadence. It was bliss beyond his wildest dreams.

Hours later, when Kiely woke, Cooper was gone. She missed him, and that surprised her. She had never missed any man before. But now she was missing him, missing his touch, and the scent of his cologne that wafted from room to room. The night between them had been exquisite. It had been more than she could have ever imagined. She couldn't see herself ever being with any other man ever again. Cooper had claimed her, body and soul, and he had a grip on her heart that was irrefutable.

Movement out of the corner of her eye pulled at her attention. Alfie had crawled up on the bed and sat on the pillow beside her, calling her name. He patted her face and lifted one eyelid and then the other. "Mornin', Ki-Ki!"

"Good morning, Alfie!" She gave him a hug.

"Alfie cuddle with Ki-Ki," he said as he snuggled with her beneath the covers.

She reached for the television remote and found the local PBS affiliate, playing an episode of *Sesame Street*. Alfie was excited to see Big Bird skipping across the television screen that hung on the wall. His joyous laugh rang through the room. Kiely laughed with him. It was going to be that kind of day for the two of them.

# Chapter 11

Cooper entered the FBI office like a man on a mission, a pep to his step. Claire Miller stepped into his office, her brows raised.

"Good morning, Agent Winston!"

"Agent Miller, it's good to see you!"

"It's good to see you, too! You're looking all spry this morning. I thought you were still out on medical leave?"

"Technically, I am, but the mayor wanted to tear me a new one this morning."

"He's been here twice this week looking for a victim. Personally, I would have stayed in my sickbed. No point in just giving him a target to kick."

"What can I say? I'm a glutton for punishment."

"I keep warning you, that martyr complex of yours is going to be your downfall."

Cooper laughed. "Hard head, soft ass, what can I say!"

"Seriously though, why are you here? I know good and well you haven't been approved to come back yet."

"We got a tip on Landon Street. I want to personally vet it."

"So, if you couldn't vet it remotely, that means you plan to go out in the field."

"Unless you tattle on me."

"I'm no snitch as long as I can ride shotgun. You might need backup and I'm a better shot than you are."

"You are never going to let me forget that, are you?"

"The truth sometimes hurts, my friend!"

Cooper nodded. "I'd appreciate your help in case things go left. If we can get this monster off the streets it'll be worth the hurt I'm going to feel later."

"You mean when Ms. Colton finds out what you're up to?"

He lifted his brows and deliberately widened his eyes. "I don't know what you're talking about."

Claire laughed. "I saw how you two were looking at each other. Now you come skipping into the office like it's Christmas Day and you got all the presents you wanted. Clearly, protective custody with a beautiful woman becomes you."

Cooper laughed with her. He felt himself blush. "Ms. Colton and I are just friends and she's been a great help to me."

"It's your lie, tell it any way you want to," Claire said matter-of-factly.

He shook his head, changing the subject. "I'm ready to roll when you are. Carter and Jones are coming with us."

"Give me ten and make sure you put on a vest. If you get shot again, Kiely will kill both of us."

Cooper laughed. "You got that right!"

After rounding up the team, doing a weapons check and making sure everyone was tactically equipped, it was Cooper riding shotgun as Claire drove to the College Avenue location in South Hills. The residence was a single-family, Tudor-style Craftsman in a meticulously maintained neighborhood. The property was currently owned by the bank, having been foreclosed on months earlier. Anyone living there did so without permission.

Their two black Suburbans pulled into the home's driveway. The grass was freshly cut, but the mailbox overflowed, envelopes and coupon flyers littering the porch. There was a Realtor's security box on the doorknob and a call to the listing agent gave them the code.

Two agents covered the back of the home and Cooper led the way through in. He announced them as he threw the front door open, his weapon raised.

Claire banked left through the dining room and Cooper went right toward the kitchen. When the first floor was clear, Claire opened the door to the other agents who scaled the second floor.

It took no time at all to assess that the home was empty, no sign of life to be found. Cooper secured his weapon. His frustration was palpable, feeling like he'd wasted time they didn't necessarily have.

Agent Miller suddenly called his name. "You need to see this," she yelled from the lower level.

Cooper descended the steps to find a makeshift lab in the basement. Bunsen burners, glass beakers and vials of chemicals littered a folding table that sat in the center of the room. A small cot and a sleeping bag rested in a far corner and an oversized garbage container was filled with empty cola cans, Cracker Jack boxes, and Kashi granola containers.

"He was here," Claire said. "I've already called for a forensics team but I'm betting this is ricin," she said as they appraised a tray of powder and a jar of castor beans.

Cooper barked out orders. "Talk to the listing agent. I want a list of everyone who requested access to this house. Names, addresses, contact information. And I want to know everything you can find out about the agent on record. If they're not showing this house I want to know why. I want to know how Street was able to set up shop down here and go undetected. I also want a team on surveillance. If he comes back we better know it. And find out who's cutting the damn lawn! I want to know who's been maintaining the property."

A round of "yes, sirs" responded back.

Cooper headed back up the steps, following behind Claire who led the way.

"We'll get him. I'll make sure they go through this house with a fine-tooth comb," she was saying. "I'll keep you updated."

"I appreciate that. I hate we didn't get him this time."

"You know how this goes, Cooper. Sometimes it takes the extra effort for us to get to the rewards."

Cooper nodded. "I appreciate you, Agent Miller."

She smiled. "Your ride's waiting for you. Tell Kiely I said hello."

Cooper dozed lightly as a junior agent drove him back to the safe house. What he hadn't gotten was a lot of sleep the night before and the memories of why had him grinning from ear to ear. Making love to Kiely had been an unexpected blessing and they'd made love multiple times before the sun rose. She'd been sound asleep when the car and driver had arrived to pick him up for his morning meeting with the mayor. Watching her he hadn't wanted to leave and now he was excited to get back to her and Alfie.

Making love to her had confirmed that she had his heart on lock. He couldn't begin to imagine what it might be like to not have her in his life and all he wanted to think about was what their future would look like. Between their sexual escapades they had talked about their dreams, their aspirations and their fears. He'd shared things with Kiely that he had never shared with anyone.

Kiely knew he was petrified of failing his son. Kiely knew he wanted to be a better man for Alfie than his own father had been for him. Kiely knew he struggled with balancing work and family. Kiely knew his heart more than anybody else. He had allowed himself to be vulnerable and he had let her in. The entire experience had been transformative, and the loneliness he had often felt was gone.

Kiely's fears mirrored his own. She'd told him that she worried about not being able to make true connections. She was afraid of the walls that she placed in relationships and around her heart. Kiely was scared that pushing people away would leave her alone in her old age. And Kiely had opened up and shared those fears with him. Kiely had let him into her heart and her head, trusting him with her secrets and her body.

Cooper had one regret. He had not shared the depths of what he was feeling. He hadn't been able to say those three words. They had vibrated loudly in his head, but he hadn't been able to speak them out loud. He found himself excited at the prospect of telling Kiely that he loved her.

When the car pulled into the driveway, Cooper

barely said his goodbyes before jumping out and racing to the front door. He gave the agent a quick wave of his hand and moved inside, locking the door securely behind him.

"Daddy's home!" he yelled.

"Daddy's home!" Kiely responded as she and Alfie came to greet him.

Alfie clapped his hands excitedly. "Dad-dy! Dad-dy! Alfie played outside. And me painted a picture. Then me cooked dinner with my Ki-Ki!" He took a breath and laughed, tossing up his hands gleefully.

Cooper scooped the child up into his arms. "Oh my! It sounds like you and Kiely had a day!"

Kiely pressed her palm to his chest and reached to kiss his lips. "How was your day?"

"It wasn't nearly as eventful as your day sounds."

"We had a great day. Are you hungry?"

Cooper nodded. "I am but I thought I would give you a break and spend some time with Alfie before we put him down to bed."

Kiely smiled. "He's missed you."

"Did you miss me?"

She kissed him again. "As soon as Alfie goes to sleep, I'll show you how much I missed you!"

Alfie toddled happily around the small bedroom showing Cooper the toys that he was most enamored with. The two chattered like old men, mumbling nonsensically and laughing at everything. It wasn't lost on Cooper that times like this with his son were priceless and he had missed too many hours consumed by a case when he should have been focused on his child. He promised Alfie to do better. It was barely thirty minutes later when the little boy fell asleep in his lap. They had been reading Alfie's favorite book for the fourth time.

After tucking him in his bed, Cooper moved to the master bedroom to grab a quick shower. By the time he finished, changing into sweats and a T-shirt, Kiely was putting their dinner on the table.

"Something smells really good," he said.

"Lasagna with ground sausage and turkey and my mother's marinara sauce."

"You really love to cook, don't you?"

"I do," Kiely answered. "More than I realized."

She stood in the kitchen tossing a salad in a wooden salad bowl. Cooper eased behind her and kissed her neck. She turned her head to meet his lips, his mouth lingering against hers. Fighting the urge to lay her across the kitchen counter and cover every inch of his maleness with the softness of her femininity, Cooper found himself struggling to maintain some self-control. He turned his back to her, reaching for a glass out of the cupboard to hide the rise of his erection.

"How did your meeting with the mayor go?" Kiely questioned, seeming oblivious to his situation.

Cooper shrugged, his shoulders jutting toward the ceiling. "He's not happy and he wants to make sure no one else is either. I was able to talk him out of a press conference though."

"I thought you would have been back earlier."

"I stopped by the office and then I went on a raid," he said, avoiding her eyes as the words came out of his mouth.

"Really, Cooper? Didn't the doctor tell you to stay out of the field for six weeks?"

"We got a tip on Landon Street. I couldn't let that go. You would have done the same thing."

"Yeah, I probably would have." She nodded. "So, anything come of it?"

"No, it was a bust. He wasn't there. But he had been there and he'd set up a lab. We're trying to figure out now what he was up to."

"I spoke to Sadie this morning."

"How's she doing?"

"She's sad. And she's still having a hard time believing that Tate's a criminal."

"I'm sorry about that."

"She'll be fine. Sadie's a smart woman. She has always dealt in fact. The evidence against him is substantial and she's been reading through it all."

Cooper nodded. "We'll find him, too." He finished the last bite of his lasagna. "Dinner was very good," he said.

"Dessert will be better."

"Should I even ask?"

They talked for some time, comparing notes and catching up. Cooper was fully engaged when Kiely shared Alfie's accomplishments. His son was becoming quite the acrobatic daredevil, climbing trees without a care in the world.

When the meal was done, he pointed her in the direction of the living room. "I'll do the dishes, you take a break."

"Are you sure?"

Cooper nodded. "I've got this."

Minutes later Kiely lay with her eyes closed, her relaxed body sprawled against the sectional cushions in wild abandon. Thoughts of Cooper danced behind her eyes. Her full breasts pushed against the cotton fabric of her silky T-shirt, and the slight curve of her buttocks peeked past the hemline of the matching shorts she wore.

Moving into the room Cooper stopped to watch her. He was enamored with the harmony that shadowed her expression. He took a deep breath and inhaled her beauty. Kiely was breathtaking and Cooper was suddenly consumed by the heat that rushed from one end of his body to the other. He shivered with longing, scarcely able to restrain himself. Her name caught in his throat as he whispered it into the warm air, the lilt of it resonating throughout the room.

Kiely rose up onto her elbows meeting his gaze.

It suddenly felt like he'd lit a fire within her, causing her to melt like butter. She could feel the swell of her breathing mirroring his own, could feel herself beginning to perspire as she stared up at Cooper. Tiny beads of moisture were forming in the valley between her breasts and she was fearful that she might break out into a full sweat. Cooper crawled over her, hovering easily above the length of her body. The moment felt unreal, like a sweet dream that had blossomed from many years of fantasy. His lips skated across hers, his tongue anxious and probing. Heat pulsed with a vengeance through her most private place.

Pressing her palms to Cooper's chest, Kiely followed as he eased her back against the sofa, reclining his weight against her. The reality of the promises they had made to each other, his heart in exchange for hers, suddenly filled her abundantly. Kiely wrapped her arms around him, her hands racing the length of his broad back. His skin was warm, the rising heat of his body simmering beneath her fingertips.

Cooper whispered her name against her skin, blowing promises with every kiss that touched her. His caresses were like feathery lashes against her skin and made her nerve endings tingle with anticipation. He suddenly sat back on his haunches, lifting the bulk of his weight from her as he stared down into the depths of her eyes. She could feel his heart beating in perfect sync with hers. Her breathing was static, desire desperate for oxygen. Kiely pulled her hands through her hair, her back arching ever so slightly. His lips searched the length of her neck, probing at the lobe of her ear before falling back to her mouth.

He undressed her slowly, pulling at her top, and she lifted her arms high above her head. The feel of his hands as he reached to cup her breasts, his palms dancing across the hardened nipples, flooded her body with sensation. His touch fired energy in the top of her head straight down to her curled toes. When his mouth followed where his hands had led, it left her breathless. Cooper was in full control as he guided her in an erotic two-step across the cushions.

Cooper tasted every square inch of her body with his own. It was pleasure beyond his wildest imagination. Kiely was completely lost in the ecstasy, sensual pleasure like a trusted tour guide. Savoring the enormity of the moment, both knew they had reached a point of no return.

"I love you," Cooper whispered into her ear as they climaxed together. "I love you, Kiely Colton."

Kiely whispered back, "I love you, too."

Kiely felt rested even though she had only gotten a few hours of sleep. She eased her body from the bed, taking care not to disturb Cooper. He lay flat on his stomach with his arms curled over his head and gripping the pillow, snoring softly. He wouldn't admit it, but she could tell the previous day had been more than he was ready to handle. He hurt and didn't want to say so. But she was learning how to read him and his many moods. She knew he needed rest and their late-night antics were proving to be a disruption.

It was still very early in the morning. With luck, she had another two hours before Alfie would wake seeking her attention. She wanted to use those two hours wisely. She was hoping that she'd see her twin later that day and she needed to send Pippa an updated shopping list before she arrived. She also wanted to check her email and answer her messages. Despite her best efforts to be a superhero, Kiely had let some of her business responsibilities slide. She also couldn't remember if she'd made her car loan payment.

Rising from the bedside she headed into the bathroom and turned on the shower. In no time at all the hot water was calling her name. As she stood in the flow she made a list of things to do in her head but was pleasantly surprised when Cooper suddenly joined her.

"Good morning! I hope I didn't wake you?"

"No," Cooper said. "I woke up, and you weren't there. I missed you."

"Join me?" she asked.

Stepping cautiously behind her, Cooper eased in, moving to stand beneath the water. The shower was oversized and they both fit in nicely. The spray was heated and comforting. Cooper pressed his hand to her back, massaging a bar of soap against her skin. Suddenly Kiely could focus on nothing but the heat from his fingertips radiating through her.

Cooper's touch was electric, burning with fierce intensity. He drew a slow trail across her shoulders, down the length of her arms, to the curve of her breasts. He continued past her belly button, and finally rested his hand teasingly against the flat of her stomach.

Kiely backed up and fit tightly against him, caressing him in a slow grind. Spinning in his arms her hands danced like butterflies over his chest and around to his broad back. Cooper pressed a kiss to her mouth, greedily sneaking his tongue past the line of her lips. The kiss was hard and deep and when Kiely finally pulled away she could barely breathe from the sheer beauty of it.

Kiely laughed softly, dropping her forehead against his chest. "If we keep this up we're going to drown in here. We're also not going to get anything accomplished."

Cooper pulled her hand to his lips and kissed the tips of her fingers. "We should spend the whole day in bed together."

"Good luck with that. I'm sure Alfie has other plans for our day today."

"Twenty questions," Cooper said. "What's your dream vacation destination?"

"Spain. I want to see La Sagrada Familia Church in Barcelona. How many stamps do you have in your passport?"

"About a dozen."

"Whoo! That's really good." They were still lathering each other, spreading soap suds with their fingertips. "Who's your favorite singer?"

"Tim McGraw."

"Country music! I'm very impressed."

"Why do you say it like that?"

"For some reason I took you for a Wayne Newton fan."

"I like Wayne Newton, too!"

Kiely rolled her eyes skyward. "Ask a question."

"What's wrong with Wayne Newton?"

She laughed. "Not a thing if that's what you like." She jumped when his fingers grazed her nether regions, his expression smug. "What's your most sensitive body part?" she said.

There was a moment of hesitation. Cooper shook his head. "No, it was my turn to ask a question."

"You did," Kiely responded. "What's wrong with Wayne Newton?" Her tone was mocking and they both laughed.

"That's not fair. That wasn't my question."

"You asked it. Now answer my question, what's your most sensitive body part?"

Cooper licked his lips as he considered his response.

"Oh, forget it!" Kiely exclaimed. "I already know the answer." She wrapped her fingers around his manhood and gave it a gentle squeeze.

Cooper inhaled swiftly. "That wasn't my answer," he said.

Kiely giggled. "I know!" And then she licked his nipple, sucking him gently.

Cooper jumped, gasping. He moaned. Loudly. "You really don't play fair," he managed to mutter.

"What's that old saying?" Kiely quipped. "All's fair in love and love."

# *Chapter 12*

Cooper and Alfie played a rousing game of hide-and-seek that afternoon. Alfie loved hiding, popping out when he felt you were taking too long to find him. Kiely knew all of his favorite hiding spots, but Cooper was completely lost as he threw open closet doors and looked under the beds. He moved back into the family room, confusion washing over his face. Kiely laughed heartily and pointed to the ottoman in the center of the floor. The top to the storage unit was askew, and if you looked closely you could see the child peeking out at the two of them. His father shook his head.

"Kiely, I can't find Alfie. I don't know where he is," Cooper said loudly.

Alfie jumped from his hiding space. "Boo!" he yelled, laughing hysterically.

Cooper clutched his chest. "Alfie! There you are, son!" He lifted the boy into the air and spun him around. "You are such a good hider, Alfie."

Once his little feet were firmly planted back on the ground Alfie ran to Kiely's side. "Dad-dy no find me, Ki-Ki! Alfie hide good!"

"Yes, you did, precious!" She knelt down to give him a hug. "Do you want to color a picture now?"

"No! Alfie go hide!" he said as he turned, racing off in the other direction. "Find me, Dad-dy! Find me!"

Kiely laughed. "Go find him, Daddy. He'll be in the clothes hamper in the laundry room."

"Will he do this all day?"

"He will do it until you make him stop." She checked the time. "You're in luck. *Daniel Tiger's Neighborhood* starts in five minutes. Daniel Tiger is one of his favorites," she said.

"Daniel Tiger?"

Kiely laughed again. "Don't ask. It's one of his favorite shows."

"How do I not know this?" Cooper muttered.

"You better count. He doesn't like it when you don't count."

Cooper shook his head. "One, two, three, four…" He moved down the hallway toward the laundry room.

Kiely was enjoying their time together. Cooper had finally slowed down long enough to enjoy his time with Alfie. He was relaxed and happy. And so was she. The dynamics of their relationship had shifted substantially. Cooper loved her and she loved him. Now she understood how Pippa had felt when Emmanuel had stolen her heart. Love didn't hurt and instead of being afraid for the future it made you hopeful. Unlike how Sadie had acted with Tate, Kiely couldn't begin to imagine Cooper bullying or trying to control her. Love didn't throw harsh words or impose rigid rules on a person's dreams.

In the other room she could hear Cooper and Alfie laughing together excitedly. She knew that his father finding him had gone well and pure joy rang out in Alfie's giggles. Kiely moved to the pantry, studying the inventory that was waning substantially. They were low on snacks for Alfie and the supply of baking ingredients was almost nonexistent. She added flour and chocolate chips to her shopping list. Moving to the freezer she checked the frozen items and ticked off vegetables and ice cream on her list.

Minutes later she emailed the list to Pippa, excited that she was going to be able to see her sister later that afternoon. She missed her family. She missed her brothers being annoying. She missed the camaraderie and laughter that she shared with her sisters. She also missed her cat, Jim Morrison.

She smiled, excited that she would soon be able to introduce Jim and Alfie, knowing the two would become fast friends.

Minutes later Cooper returned to the family room. "Finally!" he said as he dropped down onto the sectional sofa. "He's in our bed watching that Tiger kid show."

"Daniel Tiger is actually very educational," Kiely said. "You should watch it."

"I have a boatload of paperwork to get through. I need to head downstairs and see where we're at with the case."

"Do you need any help?"

"No, but thank you for offering. I need to file my report on the Landon Street debacle, and that won't take long."

"Well, if you don't need me, I think I'm going to make challah."

"You know how to make challah? From scratch?"

"Is there any other way to make challah?" she said with a wry laugh.

Cooper laughed with her. "Yeah! You let a bakery do it for you. Wealthy Street Bakery has some of the best I've ever eaten."

She smirked. "Their bread is good, but mine is better. I do like their cinnamon croissants, though."

"Townies! Those things are incredible!"

Alfie suddenly cried out, racing back into the room, tears streaming down his little face. He held his finger out, his wrist resting in the palm of his other hand.

"What's the matter, son?" Cooper questioned, moving toward the child.

Alfie snatched his hand from his father's reach, giving him a mean side-eye. He darted past him and rushed to Kiely. "Ki-Ki! Hurt my finger!" he cried.

"What am I?" Cooper exclaimed, "chopped liver? Did you see the look he just gave me?"

Kiely giggled. She brought herself to his eye level as Alfie bumped against her leg.

"My poor baby! Let Kiely see." Kiely inspected the appendage, declaring the small scratch minor. "It's going to be okay, Alfie. Do you want Kiely to kiss it or put a Band-Aid on it?"

"Alfie want a Band-Aid."

Kiely tickled him, making the little boy laugh. "Kiely's going to kiss that finger," she teased. She kissed the back of his hand then blew a strawberry against his palm. Alfie erupted in giggles.

"Snack, peas? Alfie want a snack, peas!"

In no time at all, a major meltdown had been avoided and Alfie was settled back in front of the television with a small bowl of popcorn and a juice pack.

"He really adores you," Cooper said.

"Does that bother you?" Kiely questioned. "Because I don't want you to think that I'm trying to take your place or replace his mother."

"Not at all. I'm glad he has you. I know how much you care for him," Cooper said. "May I ask you a question?"

"Of course," Kiely answered. "You know you can ask me anything."

"How do you see things once we go back to reality? When we return to our homes?"

Kiely paused. "I'm not sure. I've thought about it but I don't have a cut and dry answer."

Cooper took a seat at the kitchen table. "I've actually been thinking about that a lot. Trying to figure out how Alfie and I can keep you." His eyes smiled as he stared at her.

Kiely lifted her lips in a smile. "There's so much we have to figure out, because in all honesty, I don't know that I want to go back to being a full-time investigator. I've really come to love being a stay-at-home mom." There was a hint of nervousness that crossed her face as she made the admission.

Cooper's gaze skated across her face. He nodded his head. "We'll have to make some serious decisions about our future living arrangements."

"We're going to have to make some serious decisions about everything," Kiely responded.

Cooper crooked his fingers and beckoned her to his side. When she stood beside him, he pulled her down onto his lap, his arms wrapped tightly around her. "Kiely, you make me happier than I have been in a very long time. I don't want to lose you. And

I don't want Alfie to lose what you and he have to-gether. You've become as important to my son as you are to me. We will make this work."

He kissed her lips and tightened the hold he had around her torso. Kiely wrapped her arms around his neck and hugged him back. It suddenly felt like Christmas in July!

Cooper was still in the basement office and Alfie was down for his afternoon nap when Pippa arrived. The two sisters hugged tightly as Kiely welcomed her into the home.

"This is cute!" Pippa said, her gaze sweeping through the space. "The FBI do things with style!"

"It's comfortable."

"Where is everybody?" Pippa asked, her voice dropping an octave.

"Cooper's downstairs and Alfie's still sleeping."

"I guess you're going to have to help me with these bags then," Pippa said as she turned, heading back to the car.

Kiely slipped on her loafers and followed her sister. "What do we owe you?" she asked as Pippa handed her two oversized cloth bags filled to the brim with foodstuffs.

"Nothing. Cooper gave me his business credit card."

"When did you see Cooper?"

"He stopped by the other safe house to check on

Sadie. We really like him!" she exclaimed. "You done good this time!"

"He never mentioned it," Kiely said, suddenly wondering what else Cooper had conveniently forgotten to tell her.

"I don't think it was a secret, Kiely. He was genuinely concerned about Sadie and he said that you were upset that you couldn't be there for her so he wanted to assure her everything would be alright. He also had questions for her about Tate and wanted to answer any questions she might have had. After he left she actually perked up a bit. She agrees that he's perfect for you!"

Kiely gave her sister a look. "He told me he loves me."

Pippa grinned. "And what did you say?"

"I told him I loved him, too!"

"Maybe we can have a double wedding!" Pippa said excitedly.

"I don't know if I want to get married," Kiely confessed. "Why do I need a sheet of paper to legitimize what we feel for each other?"

"Why are you always so contrary?"

"I'm not. I just don't think I need a license to tell me that I love him and he loves me and we want to spend our lives together."

"And how does Cooper feel about that?"

"We haven't had that conversation yet."

Pippa shook her head. "Well, you do keep things interesting."

Kiely laughed.

"I brought you a surprise," Kiely said. "Grab the box on the back seat."

Opening the rear passenger door to peer inside, Kiely's eyes widened. "You didn't?"

Pippa nodded. "I did. I figured you might need it right about now!"

Cooper suddenly called from the open door. "Hey there! Do you two need some help?"

"Yes!" Kiely yelled as he moved toward them. "I need you to get this box off the back seat and do not drop it."

Cooper laughed, eyeing the Greek to Go label on top of the large white bakery box. "What's this?"

Kiely grinned. "The best baklava cheesecake you will ever experience. Take it inside and put it carefully on the counter!"

Cooper carried the cake inside, his viselike grip on the box moving both women to laugh jovially. The twins were suddenly giddy with laughter.

"You put the coffee on," Pippa said. "I'll cut the cake."

Kiely laughed. "We have a Keurig brewer. The coffee will be done before you get the first slice on a plate."

Pippa moved ahead of her through the doorway.

Kiely suddenly came to an abrupt stop, cocking

her head as she listened. They had become accustomed to the silence, anything stirring between the trees, chirping or squeaking as the wind blew. For a split second she thought she heard an engine running but just like that the sound disappeared. She set the two grocery bags against the landing and moved back down the steps to look around. Nothing caught her eye or seemed out of place. The trike Alfie had ridden earlier was still resting where he'd left it and nothing moved beyond the line of trees bordering the home. Kiely took a deep breath and held it.

"Everything okay?" Cooper asked, standing in the doorway staring at her.

"I thought I heard something," she said.

He moved down the steps to stand beside her. His gaze followed hers, searching where she looked. "Do you still hear it?" he asked.

Kiely shook her head. "No. It was probably just the wind."

He nudged her shoulder. "Let's go inside," he said as they moved back up the stairs. He grabbed the two bags of groceries.

They both tossed one last look over their shoulders and then locked the door behind themselves.

Alfie stood an arm's length away from Pippa. He stared intently, playing a game of eye ping-pong as he shifted his gaze back and forth between her and Kiely.

"He is so funny," Pippa laughed.

"He's trying to figure out why you look like me," Kiely said.

"I know you two are fraternal twins, but you do look very much alike. I can just imagine he's having a hard time processing why," Cooper interjected.

Alfie moved back to Kiely's side, the look he gave Pippa moving them all to laugh. Kiely lifted him to her lap. She ran her fingers through his hair. Alfie reached for her fork, wanting another bite of the cake that she'd been coveting.

"I think we have another convert," Pippa said.

Cooper took his own bite, swirling the taste across his tongue. The New York style cheesecake made with Greek yogurt had a walnut and cinnamon baklava filling encased in filo dough and drizzled with honey. It was everything Kiely had asserted, the decadence unrivaled by any other cheesecake he'd ever eaten. "I can't blame him," he said. "This is so good!"

"There are rules about when we can and can't eat this cake," Pippa said.

Kiely nodded. "We only eat this cake once per month."

"Also, on holidays, stress days and for special celebrations."

"The third Friday of every month."

"And every other Tuesday."

The sisters laughed.

"So, pretty much any time you want. Is that what I'm understanding?" Cooper said.

"I like him. He's smart," Pippa teased.

Kiely tossed him a look. "I'm sure he has moments."

"Okay! On that note, I am officially out of my depth. Time to retire to the other side." Cooper stood up. "Alfie, do you want to go outside and play with Daddy?"

"Alfie go outside," the little boy said. He gave Kiely a hug before jumping from her lap.

"Can I have a hug, too?" Pippa asked.

Alfie's smile fell into a deep frown. "You not my Ki-Ki," he said.

The two women watched as he stomped past Pippa, moving to Cooper's side. When his father had his hand, he tossed Pippa a look over his shoulder.

"I think he just gave you a middle-finger salute," Kiely said.

"I don't think I got a full finger wave. More like a little finger," Pippa joked. "That kid is so darn cute! And look at you being all mommy-like! Who are you and what did you do with my twin sister?"

Laughter was loud and raucous. "I like this mommy gig. More than I thought I ever would."

"Clearly! I'll be honest. We all thought it was just a phase. That by the second day you would have been ready to pull your hair out, or Cooper would find his kid stuffed in a closet."

"It's definitely not a phase. I don't know if I want to continue doing PI work full time. I think I want to be a more of a stay-at-home mom. Is that crazy?"

Pippa shook her head. "Not really. The risk factor in both is about the same."

Kiely laughed. "You might be right about that."

Cooper stared out over the backyard. Alfie was digging a hole with a large stick. He was playing happily, oblivious to anything the adults around him might have been going through. He found himself thinking about what Kiely might've heard earlier. The area was pretty remote and had been chosen for a reason. There was a team in close proximity if they were ever needed. Agents could be there before they hung up the line. Although it appeared they were alone and might be hampered without transportation, such was farthest from the truth. Cooper hadn't intended for them to be bait; he knew that if that woman came for him, or his son, again, he would be more than ready for her.

He would check later to see if any of the agents had been out in the woods patrolling the area. He knew they would occasionally check the property in stealth mode so as not to be seen. They were undoubtedly good at what they did; they had strict instructions to stay at least sixty yards from the house unless the family's safety required them to be closer. He also wanted to make sure they'd found no one else on the property who wasn't supposed to be there.

Lost in thought, Cooper was halfway up the steps when he realized Alfie wasn't beside him. Turning abruptly, he tore after the child, a moment of panic sweeping through him. By the time Cooper reached the steps, Alfie was banging at the door calling for Kiely.

"Ki-Ki! Ki-Ki! Open da door, Ki-Ki! Got to go potty!"

When Kiely pulled the entrance open, Alfie tore past her, leaving Cooper standing there feeling slightly foolish.

"He ran off," Cooper said as she stared at him.

"He has to go potty," she said.

"Potty?"

"We're potty training. He likes to aim. You should know all about that. It's a boy thing."

Alfie screamed her name. "Ki-Ki!"

"That sounds like he may need help wiping," she said as she turned from the door. "That requires a little more than aim and shake."

Moving into the home Cooper gave Pippa a look, his confounded expression moving her to laugh. He shrugged his broad shoulders, feeling slightly discombobulated.

"Yeah," Pippa said. "It's like that sometimes!"

\* \* \*

Once again that night, Kiely was wrapped around a pillow and Cooper was wrapped around her. Pippa had left earlier, having already called to say she was home safe and sound. Alfie had gone down after one last slice of cheesecake. He'd played hard and was sleeping harder.

"When I looked up and he was gone, I panicked," Cooper was saying.

"He's fast. You can take your eyes off him for a split second and he'll be a mile away. I've lost him a few times myself."

"You lost my son?"

"You lost your son."

He brushed his pelvis against her buttocks. "Well, I felt wholeheartedly inadequate and then when I found out he was potty training...when did that happen?"

"We've really just started and he's pretty much training himself."

"There's so much I don't know about my son. I feel like I need to make up for a lot of lost time. It's made me realize how much I've been focused on the agency and my job the last two years instead of focusing on Alfie."

"You're here now. And Alfie is an amazing child because you have been here. I'm sure that as he gets older you'll have to be more hands-on. You'll figure it out."

"We'll figure it out together, Ki-Ki!" Cooper said, imitating how his son called her name.

She turned in his arms and pressed a kiss to his chest. They talked for a good long while, defining how they saw their future together. They were conscious of the fact that everything they decided would impact Alfie either directly or indirectly, and that he had to be in the forefront of whatever choices they made for themselves.

It was after midnight when Cooper fell asleep, slumber claiming him first. Kiely started to drift off as she settled into his light snores. She was groggy, her eyes opening and then closing. She saw a shadow moving past the window and heard a branch snapping, startling her awake so she sat upright in the bed.

She tapped Cooper awake as she slid out of the bed.

"What's wrong?" he said, rubbing his eyes.

Kiely whispered. "Someone's outside," she said, pointing toward the bedroom window.

Cooper jumped from the bed, reaching for the lock box by the bedside. Punching in the security code he retrieved his service weapon and passed Kiely her gun.

They moved through the house swiftly. Kiely hurried to the sliding glass doors in the back and Cooper opened the front door. Both eased out at the same time. At the bottom of the steps Cooper turned to the right, sweeping from one side to the other as he eased toward the end of the house and the bedroom window. Kiely's steps mirrored his as she turned left, headed in the same direction.

As they both turned the corner, they were suddenly standing in the midst of a herd of white-tail deer, some so close that they could have reached out to pet them. There were at least sixty of them of assorted ages and sizes. The air around them was still, the quiet like a thick fog around them. Just the occasional snap of a branch beneath their hoofs. There was a full moon lighting the dark sky, the bright glow illuminating the landscape. It was surreal and so breathtakingly beautiful that Kiely heard herself gasp. Realizing the threat beneath the bedroom window was only Bambi and company out for their midnight stroll, she lowered her weapon first and then Cooper dropped his arm down to his side.

The deer had bristled, heads turning in their direction, ears lifted as they measured the degree of danger to them. A few were skittish, eyes watching them cautiously. Neither Kiely nor Cooper moved, so mesmerized by the moment that they had almost forgotten why they were standing outside in the middle of the night, oblivious to everything, even the chill in the air. Almost, but not quite, acutely aware that they weren't out of the woods and a potential threat to their lives was still very real.

Finding nothing significant after one final sweep

of the property, Cooper slowly slid his weapon into the waistband of his pants. Kiely did the same thing. She held her breath when a small fawn brushed past her leg, curiosity larger than its fear. It was eerie to have them inch as close as they came, curious to know if the two were friend or foe. Kiely reached for Cooper's hand and moved closer to him. He wrapped his arms around her shoulders and held her as they stood in awe of the moment.

# Chapter 13

The next morning as they sat over a breakfast of freshly squeezed orange juice and egg casserole, Kiely said, "You were up early. Is everything okay?"

Cooper swallowed the bite of toast he'd just taken. "After last night I wanted to touch base with the backup team. Another agent and I took a walk around the property just to be safe."

"Did you find anything?"

He shook his head. "No. It was clear. Even the deer were gone."

Kiely blew a soft sigh. "Do you believe in God?" she asked, the question coming out of the blue.

Cooper nodded his head. "I do. I consider myself very spiritual, but it's been some time since I last went to church."

"Define some time."

"Sara's funeral was the last time the pastor saw me."

Kiely nodded. "I was just thinking that there was something very spiritual about our experience last night. Like God walked us into an inspiring moment to show us something magnificent."

Cooper sat back in his seat. He nodded. "I wish Alfie could have experienced that with us. If they come back we should wake him up."

"It really was spectacular. Standing there in your arms, watching them, felt so calming. I almost cried."

"Baby! Aww!"

"Almost. Don't get sappy on me, Cooper Winston."

"We were just having a moment and you ruined it."

Kiely laughed. "Your daddy has jokes, Alfie!"

Alfie giggled. "You funny, Dad-dy!"

Cooper tossed up his hands. "It looks like I am never going to win with you two."

"Nope!"

"What's on your agenda today?"

"Laundry. I've run out of underwear."

"It's not like you really need them," Cooper said, his voice dropping to a loud whisper.

"So have you," Kiely added.

He blinked. "I can see where that might be a problem for us."

"What do you have to do today?"

"I need to figure out how much longer we're going to be here."

"I was actually going to ask you that. Not that I'm complaining. I've enjoyed our time."

"I really do need to get back to work, and I imagine you want to do the same thing."

Kiely rose from her seat and reached for the dirty dishes to clear away the table. Although she had thought about their return, she hadn't truly been interested in committing to any particular day or time. "No," she finally said. "I really could care less about returning to the job. Obviously, I want to solve this case so my foster brother Brody can come home, but I'm not invested in the rest of it."

"How is your brother going to feel about that?"

"It's not my brother's life."

Cooper stole a quick glance down to his wristwatch. "Let's put this conversation on hold until later. I have a conference call in thirty minutes and I need to go prepare." He stood up from the table and leaned to kiss her lips. Alfie, who was playing with his cereal, picking out the marshmallows to eat first, gave him a wave.

The video chat to Cooper began as scheduled. When he answered, the mayor's secretary announced the call and connected them. The mayor, Grand Rapids Police Chief Andrew Fox, Lieutenant

Tripp McKellar and Detective Emmanuel Iglesias had all been patched through.

"Everybody know each other?" the mayor queried.

A collective round of *yeas* responded.

"Good, then I can dispense with the pleasantries," he snapped. "Where are we with this case? I've got people dying, the press is up my ass, and you all have no answers! Someone tell me something!"

Cooper chimed in first. "The FBI has gotten a few credible tips pointing us in the direction of Landon Street and Wes Matthews. Thus far they've continued to be one step ahead of us. The FBI continues to be committed to bringing them to justice."

"That just sounds like a load of double talk to me," the mayor said. "I need results!"

Police Chief Fox added his two cents. "I've got my best men and women on the case. We'll get these guys."

"We'll get these guys. We'll get these guys," the mayor said mockingly. "I'm tired of hearing we're going to get these guys and these guys are still out here killing people."

"I understand your frustration, Mayor," Cooper interjected. "We're equally frustrated. But I assure you, we are all giving a hundred and ten percent. There are a lot of players tied to this debacle and each of them have their own agenda which has made bringing them down difficult. But we're proud to say that we've arrested one of the Capital X henchmen and he named all of his associates. We know who was behind Capital X and we have him on our radar. I believe his arrest is imminent."

"Is that something we can announce to the media? We need to give them something!"

"I can have our communications person write up a statement for you, sir."

"Get this done," the mayor snapped one last time. "Or I'll replace the whole damn lot of you!"

Cooper disconnected the call, his frustration palpable. Had the investigation been that easy, they would've been finished by now. The mayor didn't seem to understand that the criminals who didn't want to get caught were hampering him getting the results he wanted.

The rest of the day was nondescript. Cooper spent most of it on the lower level of the home working while Kiely sorted clothes and kept Alfie entertained. When he finally emerged from the dungeon, the two were playing a game of Simon Says. Alfie was having a hard time grasping the mechanics of the game, but his enthusiasm made up for his lack of skill.

He moved to the kitchen hoping to sneak a bite of ice cream and leftover cake before dinner. He wasn't surprised to find the cake missing and barely enough ice cream left to fill an eight-ounce cup.

"Really, Kiely? You ate the cheesecake?"

She laughed. "What makes you think I ate it?"

"It's just you and me, babe, and I didn't eat it."

"Alfie, who ate the cake?" Kiely questioned.

"Simon!" He threw up his hands with a loud cheer.

"Simon who?" Cooper questioned.

"Simon Says!"

Kiely laughed. "Dinner's almost ready, Cooper. And I made brownies for dessert."

"Brownies with those little chocolate chips?"

"Lots of chocolate chips."

"As long as I get the last one I'll forgive you for eating the cheesecake," Cooper said.

Kiely laughed again. "I did not eat the cheesecake!"

"Then who ate the cheesecake, Kiely? Did the deer sneak in and eat the cheesecake?"

"No, smart-ass! I hid the cheesecake so you could have the last slice. It's in the plastic container on the top shelf of the refrigerator. Now say sorry."

Cooper gave her a slight bow. "Okay, I might've stepped in that one. I'm sorry, Kiely. Thank you."

Laughter echoed around the room. As Cooper went for the cake, Kiely moved into the kitchen to finish the dinner preparations. She and Cooper traded a quick kiss as Alfie continued to run and play, making up his own game of hide-and-seek and Simon Says. The table was set and Kiely was waiting for the pot of water on the stove to boil to cook the pasta for their spaghetti dinner.

Suddenly an explosion shattered the sliding glass doors leading from the family room out to the rear deck. It knocked Kiely off her feet and she narrowly missed fracturing her head on the edge of the marble counter. Cooper held tight to an upper shelf in the pantry as the room vibrated, soup cans sliding onto the floor.

Kiely screamed. "Alfie! Alfie!" The little boy was nowhere to be seen. Kiely raced to the back bedrooms calling his name. She and Cooper met back in the living room. "I can't find Alfie."

"He was just here!" Cooper exclaimed. "Where did he go?"

"He's probably hiding," Kiely said. "He wanted to play hide-and-seek. I'll check the laundry basket," she said.

She raced back to the laundry room and when she didn't find Alfie there, she ran back. As she moved into the space Cooper stood frozen, staring toward the shattered glass door. Her gaze shifted to where he stared, her eyes widening. Meghan Otis, the RevitaYou-taking selfie queen, stood amidst the debris of glass, metal fragments and wood slivers, pointing a gun at him. When she saw Kiely, she shifted the muzzle from him to her and back again.

She was taller than Kiely had imagined. Her body

shape was athletic and she wore biker leathers; black pants, thick-heeled boots and a jacket.

"Both of you, sit down," she said calmly.

"Who are you?" Cooper questioned, though Kiely knew he already knew the answer. He and Kiely had seen numerous photos of her and he had stalked her social media accounts until he thought he knew her well. Meghan Otis, however, had finally caught up with them and now he had to get her talking.

Meghan didn't answer his question, saying instead, "I warned you, Agent! I told you to leave Wes Matthews alone. It really didn't have to be like this!" Meghan stepped back, to peer outside. It was almost as if she were waiting for someone. She turned back to them just as quickly.

The large automatic weapon in her hands was intimidating. Both Kiely and Cooper were unnerved by how calm she was, speaking as if she were only talking about the weather and her latest Pilates class. Cooper suddenly gave Kiely a slight nod and gestured with his eyes toward the storage ottoman. Kiely realized the top was moving ever so slightly and she knew Alfie was hiding inside. She suddenly needed their baby boy to not move. To stay safe from the madwoman with the large gun who'd already kidnapped him once before. She started talking out loud, trying to keep her voice calm. "I'm counting," she said. "Kiely's counting. One, two, three, four…"

The other woman turned to stare at her. Her eyes narrowed into thin slits and she frowned. "What are you doing? I told you to sit down and shut up!"

Kiely didn't respond, eyeing the woman cautiously. "What do you want?" she finally questioned.

She pointed the gun back at Cooper. "I told him. I told him to leave Wes alone. I told him and he wouldn't listen. I told him. Now, you all are going to have to pay. Where's the kid?"

"Meghan, why don't we talk about this?" Cooper said, his tone equally as calm.

"No!" the woman snapped. She began pacing the floor, muttering under her breath. "I told you what to do. I told you! Now look what you made me do," she ranted. Her voice rose and fell from a yell to a whisper. Meghan Otis appeared to be coming unhinged right before their eyes.

Cooper shot Kiely another look, the top to the ottoman beginning to quiver a second time. "Still counting," Kiely said. "Six, seven, eight…"

Meghan suddenly stopped staring directly at Kiely, turning her attention back to Cooper. "I said, where is he?"

"Where is who?"

"The little boy."

"What do you want, Meghan? How can we help you?" Cooper asked, trying to shift her focus again.

"I told you how to help me. I told you to leave Wes alone."

"You're in love with Wes, aren't you?" Kiely questioned. "Did he hurt you, Meghan?"

Megan stopped pacing once again, turning to stare at Kiely. "Yes, I do love him. And he loves me. Everything was perfect. We were so good to-gether. We were making money. Living well." She shook the gun at Cooper. "And then he had to go and mess everything up!"

"How did he do that?" Kiely questioned. "How did Agent Winston mess things up?"

Meghan sighed, seeming relieved to be able to tell someone her story. To make sure they knew what had gotten her there and how she had found herself in the predicament she was in.

She began to talk. "Wes and I met at the bank where I used to work. I was a teller and he would come to my window and flirt with me. It was love at first sight." Meghan smiled at the memories. "One day he invited me to lunch. He was such a roman-tic! When he found out I'd recently come into some lottery money, he offered me the opportunity to in-vest in his business. Wes was quite the business-man!" Meghan exclaimed. "And the product was amazing! I used it myself and it worked wonders. I looked years younger. My skin was vibrant and the wrinkles practically faded overnight. My hair grew in thicker and I had the energy level of a woman half my age. In fact, I was able to drop twenty-five pounds that Wes thought I needed to lose. The weight just fell off! It was as if time turned back ten years."

"So, yeah," she continued, "I invested. Who wouldn't invest in something that was going to revolutionize the wellness industry! Sales were spectacular and then Wes asked me to partner with him. He said I was his good luck charm. I became his golden girl, recruiting others to come in and invest as well. The media keeps saying Wes scammed people out of their money, but he didn't do that. I made all my money back and then some. And I wasn't the only one."

Cooper shook his head. "Wes paid you back with the money he took from the investors who came after you, Meghan."

"No, he didn't," she snapped. "RevitaYou was doing well. The company was making tons of money. You don't know! I saw the books. I was there helping Wes build the brand." She stepped closer, shaking the gun in Cooper's face for emphasis.

She took a step back, inhaling deeply to calm her rage. She narrowed her gaze on Cooper. "You did that press conference. You called Wes a con man and a thief. You lied and told people the product was tainted. I'm proof there's nothing wrong with the product! Then you said you were going to bring Wes down and I couldn't let that happen. I have to protect Wes, no matter what it takes."

"So, you kidnapped my son."

"He was going to be my insurance policy. But then..." She hesitated, falling into thought. She began to slap the side of her leg with the gun, her frustration rising with a vengeance.

"I'm sorry," Cooper said.

"You're sorry!" Meghan spun toward the door and back to him a second time. "You're sorry? If you had been sorry you would have stopped. You got lucky when you rescued your kid and you didn't die when I shot you. But instead of walking away, you kept digging."

"So, you set those bombs off at my house?"

"I sent you a message," she snapped. She moved back to the door.

"Who made the bombs for you, Meghan?" Cooper questioned.

The woman gave him a look that spoke volumes, her disdain for him so intense that if looks could have killed, Cooper would have died a thousand deaths. "You can learn anything you want to learn with the internet," she quipped. She turned back to peer outside.

Cooper shot Kiely another look. Alfie had slid the ottoman top over enough to peek out. He stared at them, his eyes locked on Kiely's face. Kiely was smiling. She shook her head no and pulled her index finger to her lips for him to be quiet.

"Good boys do what they're told, right, Meghan," Kiely said loudly. "Good boys sit quiet as mice. Cooper, you need to be a good boy like Alfie. Alfie's a very good boy."

"Why are you talking?" Meghan yelled. "I told you to shut up!"

Alfie appeared to settle himself lower in the storage bin and Kiely knew the woman yelling had frightened him.

"Where's that kid? I'm not going to ask you again," she screamed, stomping back to stand in front of Cooper.

"Why do you want my son?" Cooper asked. "He doesn't have anything to do with this."

"You don't deserve him. You deserve to die. He's going to need someone to take care of him when that happens. I've been a good mother. I have a son. My Neil used to be such a sweet little boy. He turned eighteen and now he's worthless like his father. He says I'm crazy. He was supposed to help me. Now I can't even trust him. He tried to turn Wes in, you know! He called your office telling you where Wes was. I can't believe he would do that to me. I was a good mother and Wes never did anything to him! He's been trying to keep me and Wes apart since day one. Neil's just jealous."

Meghan seemed to fall into thought reflecting on her child. Cooper realized it was her son Neil who had called in the tip that had led them to the property where she had been holding Alfie.

"You don't have to do this, Meghan," Cooper said. He moved as if to stand up, holding both his hands high as if he were surrendering. "Just turn yourself in."

"Sit down," Meghan hissed. She turned the gun toward Kiely. "Or I will kill her."

Cooper eased back into his seat. He knew it would only be a matter of minutes before the cavalry would be coming. He knew the explosion had triggered his team and they were already circling the property. They just needed to keep her talking. "How did you find us?" he asked.

"You're really not that smart, Agent," Meghan answered. She gestured toward Kiely. "She led me right to you."

Cooper looked confused.

"I saw her in the store buying groceries. And I followed her. She led me right here to you."

Cooper nodded as understanding washed over him. Meghan had likely mistaken Pippa for her twin sister.

"And just so you know," Meghan continued, "she's not loyal. I saw her hugged up with that detective that you've been working with. Your girlfriend here has been lying to you. I would never do something like that to my Wes. I would ride or die for Wes Matthews."

"Where is Wes now?" Kiely questioned.

"Wouldn't you like to know! He's safe. That's all that matters. Wes is safe and you can't get to him." She suddenly reached into the back pocket of her pants and pulled out two plastic zip ties, tossing them both at Kiely. "Secure his hands and then do yours. Do it now!"

"It's okay," Cooper said, the comment meant for Alfie who was peeking out again. He held out his hands, his palms together, and Kiely secured the zip ties around his wrists.

"Make them tighter," Meghan snapped.

Kiely did as she was told, securing the zip ties even tighter. She pressed her fingers against the backs of Cooper's hands. Her touch was consoling. Her hands were steady, no fear reflected in her body language. He sat back down and she turned toward Meghan. "Now what?"

"Secure your wrists, that's what!"

"I can't do my own hands," Kiely said.

Frustration furrowed Meghan's brow. "You can and you will!" She took two fury-filled steps toward Kiely.

As she closed the distance between them, Kiely sprang into action. Meghan wasn't expecting the karate kick that landed in her chest. As she fell backward, Kiely slammed her a second time, dislodging the gun from her hands. When it fell to the floor Cooper lunged for it. Meghan scrambled to her feet faster than Kiely had anticipated. She also dove for the weapon, but Kiely blocked her. The two women were suddenly trading blows, each punch harder than the last. Going toe to toe, Meghan landed a blow that dropped Kiely to her knees.

At that moment, Alfie sprang out from the ottoman, tears streaming down his little face. He screamed Kiely's name, crying hysterically. "Ki-Ki! Ki-Ki!"

Meghan's eyes widened at the sight of him. It proved to be just enough of a distraction when Cooper reached the gun, took aim and fired.

# *Chapter 14*

Kiely sat on the front porch of the home rocking Alfie in her lap. It had been a good two hours since those shots were fired and the little boy was still traumatized. After being reassured that he'd been a very good boy to do what Kiely had wanted of him, he'd finally stopped crying, sitting quietly with his thumb in his mouth.

Inside, Meghan Otis was dead. The threat to Cooper and his family no longer existed. One piece of the larger puzzle had been found. Agents continued to traipse in and out of the house. They had finally breached the entrance just as Cooper had discharged that weapon. In the mayhem that followed Kiely had grabbed Alfie, using her body to shield him from any harm and the sight of the dead woman lying on the floor. Now, Kiely was ready to take him back to Grand Rapids and home.

Cooper stood in the doorway watching the two of them. Kiely had refused medical attention. "It's only a black eye," she had said. "It's not my first and it and the bruises will eventually go away."

"I just want to be…" he had started.

"Just make sure Alfie isn't injured," she said, interrupting his comment. "There was a lot of glass flying and that explosion may have hurt his eardrums."

He stuck his hands deep into the pockets of his pants. Kiely had put herself in danger to protect his son, and him. During the commotion, he'd been petrified that anything could go horribly wrong and he could have lost her. His love for Kiely was corporeal. Thick, rich, nurturing. She'd become his lifeline. The air he needed to breathe. The sunshine that brightened each day. She loved him and he couldn't begin to fathom how he'd gotten so lucky. And most importantly, she loved his son as if Alfie were her own.

Watching her hold him in her lap, her arms protective vises to keep him safe from harm, the gentle reassurances whispered against the child's cheek, reaffirmed that fate had blessed him and his immensely. He had no intentions of letting karma take that from them.

He moved to where she sat and dropped down onto the top step beside her. Alfie tapped his arm with his foot.

"Hey," Kiely said softly. "How's it going in there?"

"They're almost done. But we're going to head out in a few minutes. I'm ready to go back home and I know you are, too. It's been a long day."

Kiely touched the bandage on his arm where he'd been cut by glass rolling on the floor. "What did the medic say about your ribs?"

"That I should take a few weeks off to heal."

Kiely laughed. "Where have I heard that before?"

Cooper wrapped an arm around her shoulder. "This isn't the most romantic time to ask you this question and I don't have a ring, but…" He moved to the step below them, dropping down onto one knee. "Will you marry me, Kiely Colton? Will you marry me and my son?"

Before Kiely could answer, another black sedan pulled in front of the home, coming to a screeching halt. Tripp, Emmanuel and Riley Colton exited the vehicle, rushing to where they sat.

Cooper shook hands with the trio.

"You all good?" Tripp questioned.

Cooper nodded. "We are."

"My guys just picked up Neil Otis for questioning. The kid is telling everything and he's given us full access to his mother's personal possessions. We might have another lead on Matthews."

"That's good work," Cooper said. He gestured to Grand Rapids' finest to follow him into the house. He leaned to kiss Kiely's cheek as he passed her.

Riley stood in front of her. His expression was intense as he debated whether to fuss at her or not.

"Hey, big brother," she said.

"Hey! You know you scared the hell out of me, right? Emmanuel called saying there had been a shooting and a woman had been killed. He didn't have any details and we knew you were up here alone."

"Sorry about that." She shifted Alfie against her lap and the child sat up straighter. He eyed Riley curiously, his gaze moving from the man's head to his toes.

"Who's this?" Riley asked. He gave Alfie a little poke with his index finger and the little boy giggled.

Kiely smiled a dazzling smile that lit up her face. "This is Alfie. He's mine. He's going to keep me!"

Riley nodded. "Okay. If it works for you, it works for me." He held out his hand. "Hey, kid! I'm Uncle Riley!"

Alfie smiled, pulling his thumb from his mouth. "Hi! My name Alfie!"

Cooper and Kiely both knew that bringing a sense of normalcy back to their lives would be the best thing for Alfie. After a quick Happy Meal dinner at McDonald's, he had fallen asleep on the ride back to Grand Rapids. By the time Riley dropped them off at Cooper's home, the kid's power nap had him wide open. His excitement was infectious as he raced from room to room, exploring the repairs and renovations, happy to be back in familiar surroundings.

Riley and Cooper stood in conversation as Kiely assessed the contents of the refrigerator and cupboards. They needed a serious food delivery; Alfie was in want of milk and snacks.

"I'll touch base with Tripp in the morning to see where we're at with Neil Otis. My office can help run down any information he gets," Riley said.

"I appreciate that," Cooper said. "I'm officially on desk duty pending the agency's investigation of the shooting."

Riley shot a look in his sister's direction. Kiely was muttering under her breath, making lists and quietly fussing about all she needed to do. He shook his head. "What did you do to her?"

"Excuse me?" Cooper looked confused.

"She's being nice. It's like she's been transformed. You didn't work some sort of Stepford Wives thing on her, did you?"

Cooper laughed. "You probably know better than I that Kiely does exactly what Kiely wants to do."

"Yeah, I do."

"Your sister is an amazing woman. I've fallen in love with her. I asked her to marry me."

"You're moving fast, aren't you?"

Cooper shrugged. "I think when you know, you know."

Riley suddenly thought about the woman he would soon be marrying. Charlize was pregnant with his baby, and he had lost much time with her, fighting what he knew. He would never want Kiely to make that mistake if Cooper was the man for her. He extended his arm to shake Cooper's hand. "I'm sure my sisters have already threatened you," he said. "Just make sure you take care of Kiely. I would hate to see them hurt you."

"She's in good hands. I promise you, I will protect her with my life." The two men shook hands one last time.

Riley sauntered to the kitchen, reaching out his arms to give Kiely a hug. "Call me if you need anything," he said.

"Thank you," Kiely said. "We do need to talk soon. I want to make some changes."

"We all need to meet in the next day or so. Let's plan on talking then?"

Kiely nodded. "I love you, Riley."

Her brother winked his eye at her. "I love you more!"

"Bye, Wi-ley!" Alfie screamed from the other

side of the room. He had stacked a pile of blocks, trying to build a fort.

Riley waved. "See you later, alligator!"

"After while, croc-dile!"

Cooper was happy to be back in his own bed. He was even happier that Kiely lay beside him. They were both still wide awake, chatting easily as they made plans for their future. Earlier, shortly after Alfie had finally fallen to sleep for the night, Cooper had dropped onto his knee a second time to ask Kiely to be his wife. This time he produced his mother's engagement ring, a family heirloom that he'd inherited after she had passed. It was a meticulously handcrafted vintage design band of solid fourteen-carat white gold with a stunning two-carat natural diamond and a trellis of diamonds cascading downward from either side.

After she had said yes, kissing him passionately, they had both called their families to give them the happy news.

"I want to hyphenate my name after we get married," Kiely was saying. "Kiely Colton-Winston. You don't have a problem with that, do you?"

"No, not at all."

"Because my father made me a Colton. That means something to me. I can't see myself ever letting that go. It's my identity, who I am. I'm the daughter of a Colton."

"Kiely, I respect that. I want you to carry my name, but I don't want you to lose your identity to do that. Colton-Winston works for me."

"Thank you. Also, I don't want a big wedding. Nothing extravagant. In fact, a civil ceremony down at Town Hall and maybe a reception in the backyard would suit me just fine. Just something very casual."

Cooper chucked. "Do you even want to wear a wedding gown?"

"Only if you insist."

He nodded. "It would be nice."

"Okay. Just for you." She lifted her lips to his and kissed him, then laid herself back down beside him. "Now, what requests do you have of me?"

"I want you to adopt Alfie. I want you to legally be his mother."

Kiely turned to eye him closely. "But... Sara..."

"Sara gave birth to him. And she died after. She will always be his mother. No one can take that from her or from him. And we will tell him about her. He will know the sacrifices she made for him to be here. But, you are the only mother he will ever know. You love him as if you had birthed him yourself. I want you and Alfie to have all the legal protections you would have if your name were on his birth certificate. I need to know that if, heaven forbid, anything ever happened to me that you will be there for Alfie. He has never been able to call anyone mommy. I want him to call you his mommy."

For the first time, in a very long time, Kiely wasn't able to hold back her tears. She cried. She cried like a baby herself. She cried to release the fear that had gripped her earlier. She cried for Meghan Otis who had loved a man unworthy of her heart. She cried for the woman's son and the pain he would now have to endure after the loss of his mother. She cried for Cooper who was trying to be a wall of strength for everyone else. She cried for Alfie and the innocence this case had tried to steal from him. She cried for Brody and all those people who'd been harmed by Wes Matthews, Landon Street and Tate Greer, and everyone else affiliated with this whole mess. And she cried for herself and the journey that had taken her far from what she imagined her life to be and had dropped her exactly where she was supposed to be.

Wiping at her eyes with the backs of her hands, she brushed her tears over her cheeks. Cooper wrapped her in his arms and held her until she was all cried out.

"I didn't mean to make you cry," Cooper said softly.

"These are happy tears," Kiely responded. "I love you so much. And I love Alfie. And I don't ever want to lose either one of you. Yes, I wouldn't hesitate to adopt him. I want to be his mother and your wife."

Kiely rolled above him, straddling her body over his. There was a long pause of silence as she stared into his eyes. When she leaned in, their lips met, barely brushing against each other before she pulled back from his touch.

Cooper eased his hands into the length of her hair and pulled her back to him. He captured her lips above his own and kissed her hard. His tongue invaded her mouth and they shared the most sensuous French kiss.

His hands wrapped around her waist, his fingers grazing the taut skin of her behind. He let go of her head and began to work the buttons on her flannel pajama top. His fingers were trembling as he undid each button, exposing her breasts. Cooper massaged one breast and then the other. As he lightly pinched and tweaked her nipples, a low moan escaped Kiely's throat.

Following suit, Kiely pulled at the string that held his pants closed and slipped her hands inside to tease the curl of pubic hair that nested his erection. Their lips met again as Cooper held her tightly to his body. He suddenly swept an arm around her waist and flipped her until her body was beneath his. He nibbled her earlobe, teasing her with his tongue. Kissing down the length of her neck, he licked and nipped at her skin, his pace slow as he explored each square inch of her.

Cooper glanced at her face. Kiely's eyes were closed and there was a beautiful smile on her face. When he sucked her nipple past his lips, she gasped. He moved from one to the other like a man starved, bringing each nipple to a peak. Cooper continued his ministrations, moving slowly down the length of her torso until he reached her feminine core.

Droplets of dew clung to the hair of her landing strip. Her sensual aroma had him brick hard, anticipation fueling the trail he left with his mouth. She squealed when he snaked his tongue into her. She spread herself open, her legs wide as he tasted her, feasting on the pinkness that lined her most private space.

He dipped and dabbled with his mouth, purposely avoiding the sensual nub as he built her up until she was desperate for release. She tasted sweet and when his tongue grazed her clit and he sucked the little nub into his mouth, Kiely arched her back and fisted the sheets beneath her.

Cooper whipped his tongue back and forth until she cried out and her juices flooded the bed beneath her buttocks. He eased himself between her legs, teasing the inner walls with his body. She met him stroke for stroke and then he felt her clench down and tighten her body around his as another orgasm ripped through her, followed closely by a third. A tear slid past her lashes as she clung to him, her nails digging into the flesh along his back. He pumped himself in and out, round and round, back and forth. When his own orgasm hit, Kiely exploded one more time, slipping sweetly with him into an erotic bliss.

The morning sunrise found them still wrapped around each other. When Kiely woke, Cooper had rolled over onto his back and she lay with half her body covering his. His morning erection beckoned for her attention. Cooper opened his eyes as she lifted herself back above him. He gasped as she plunged her body back down against his. She rotated her hips slowly against him as he reached both hands out to grasp her by the waist.

He gasped. "Good morning!"

"Good morning," she said, biting down against her bottom lip. "I thought I'd start your day off with a little dessert!"

"No wanna go to da school," Alfie said later that morning, stomping his foot at Kiely.

"Alfie, you have to go to school, precious. Your friends miss you!"

"Wanna stay wit' you, Ki-Ki!"

Cooper blew a soft sigh. Alfie had been fighting him at every step since he'd wakened. Kicking and screaming he hadn't wanted to brush his teeth, get dressed, comb his hair or eat his breakfast. Now he was adamant that he wasn't leaving the house.

Kiely sat down on the floor beside him, wrapping him in a hug. "I'll tell you what. We'll let Daddy go on to work and you and I will go to school together. I will take you to your class and when I'm done doing my work, I will come back and get you."

"Promise?"

"I promise."

"You back in two minutes, o-kay?"

Kiely smiled. "Two hours, okay?"

Alfie pondered for a moment. "O-kay." He gave his father the evil eye. "I go school wit' my Ki-Ki, Dad-dy."

Cooper laughed. "Okay, buddy!"

Alfie dashed toward the door to get his coat.

"I think it's official. He likes you more than he likes me."

Kiely laughed with him. "I have that effect on men. Especially short men who still occasionally need a diaper."

Cooper hugged and kissed her. "I should be jealous, but I get it. I like you more than I like me, too!"

"As you should," Kiely said teasingly. "Are you going into the office?"

He nodded. "I won't be there long though. All I can do is catch up on the reports and I need to sign my statement about what happened at the safe house. And since I'm technically still on medical leave, they're not going to let me stay long. What were you planning to do?"

"I'll drop Alfie off and then I need to go buy me a car. The FBI were very generous about replacing the one your suspect blew up."

"You're welcome."

She laughed. "How about I take you to lunch? I've got a taste for sushi."

Cooper frowned. "Yuck. Personally, I prefer my fish cooked."

"We're going to have to work on your palate. Meet me at Maru's on Cherry Street so I can start to school you."

"Twelve thirty?"

Kiely kissed him one last time. "Twelve thirty works for me. You ready, Alfie?"

"I going to school wit' Ki-Ki! Bye, Dad-dy! Lub you!"

Cooper laughed. "I think he's ready!"

# *Chapter 15*

Kiely had expected Alfie to put up a fuss when she dropped him off at the Goodman's Children Center. But he was excited when he saw his friends and the classroom teacher he called Miss Gee. All the children had hugged him, pulling him along to the play area and he had gone willingly once Kiely had assured him she'd be back to pick him up at the end of the day. As she exited the building the FBI agent assigned to keep an eye on Alfie gave her a nod, promising she had nothing to worry about. She didn't have the heart to tell him she would worry anyway.

The search for a new car took less than an hour.

Kiely had known before she'd left the house where she was going and what she wanted. Someone from Cooper's office had already called Toyota of Grand Rapids and a young salesman named Glenn was overly excited when she stepped through the door. Forty-five minutes later, Kiely drove off the lot with a brand-new Highlander in a loud shade of red called Ruby Pearl. After a quick stop by the local Walmart to purchase a new car seat for Alfie, Kiely headed to see her sister.

Pippa was on the phone when Kiely knocked on her office door. She waved her in as she continued her call. Taking a seat Kiely watched her twin tear into someone who hadn't done his job. When she slammed the phone receiver down, Kiely knew she had swallowed the curse word that had been on the tip of her tongue.

"Welcome home," Pippa said. She paused to jot some notes onto a pad and when she dropped the blue ink pen she turned her full attention toward Kiely. "I hear you almost got yourself killed."

"It was touch and go there for a minute."

"The black eye is pretty."

"You should see the other guy!"

Pippa shook her head. "To what do I owe the honor?"

"Wedding dresses. Where's the best place to shop for one?"

Pippa laughed. And she wouldn't stop laughing.

That hysterical laughter that only got worse when people stared or commented. When you couldn't catch your breath and it felt like the room might start to spin. Pippa laughed until tears began to roll down her face. Kiely wasn't amused.

"Why do you find that funny?"

Pippa gasped, sucking in air until she could breathe again. "Because a few days ago you were telling us you had no interest in being married. Or did you forget your 'why do I need a license to validate my relationship' speech?"

Kiely blinked. "Can't a girl change her mind?"

"You're killing me, Kiely!"

As she shrugged her shoulders, a smirky grin pulled across Kiely's face. "Give me a little credit, please. I'm here because Cooper and I would like to retain your services."

"Prenups?"

Kiely shook her head. "Adoption papers. Cooper wants me to legally adopt Alfie after we're married."

Pippa sat back in her seat, reservations simmering in her eyes. "That's a big step, Kiely. Maybe we should go back to wedding dresses. What color is your wedding party wearing? As your maid of honor, I think a mint green would be nice."

Kiely waved a dismissive hand at her sister, refocusing the conversation back on why she was there.

"I love them both so much, Pippa. It just feels right. I can't imagine *not* being Alfie's mother now."

"I have to say, watching you with Alfie and Cooper reminded me so much of how Mom had been with all of us."

"So, you'll help?"

"You know I will! But have you considered asking Griffin? Adoption is his specialty."

"I did, but with everything he and Abigail have going on I didn't want to add to his load."

"You should still ask. I think he'd appreciate it. You know he sometimes thinks we leave him out of things when that's the last thing we're trying to do. Let him say no."

Kiely nodded. "I will, but do you have any advice?"

"Personally, I would make you wait one year to officially adopt. There's going to be a lot of adjustment for you and Cooper and most especially Alfie. For now, I'd suggest you two amend your wills first and put a custody plan in place should something happen to Cooper before that year is up. You also need to consider a plan for any biological children that you two may have together, if that's something you're considering."

"That should work. Cooper and I are having lunch later. I'll tell him what you said."

Pippa's phone rang. She glanced down to the caller ID. "I need to take this. But I will call you later and we can plan on going wedding dress shopping!"

Rising from her seat, Kiely laughed. "Thank you, Pip!"

Cooper sat back in his chair, his hands folded together in his lap. He'd spent a good hour with the FBI psychologist, talking through everything that had happened. He hadn't wanted to admit that pulling the trigger and taking a woman's life had left him traumatized. Doing his job often came with regrets, but this one ran deep. Mental illness had driven Meghan Otis to do all she had done. If only her actions had not pushed them to a point of no return, helping her might have been possible.

But Cooper knew he couldn't live with second guessing his actions. Protecting his family would always be foremost in everything he did and he couldn't question choices made in the heat of a moment when they'd been in harm's way. Kiely had reminded him that talking things through would help him sleep at night. He would meet with the doctor again, for as long as he felt he needed help.

Shifting forward in his seat, he had gone through a dozen files catching up on every aspect of the case. They were getting closer to catching Wes Matthews, but they weren't there yet. The information they'd received from Neil Otis had been more than helpful. His mother had kept detailed records of her transactions with Wes. From bank accounts opened under an alias to properties purchased in the name of a shell company the FBI had been unaware of, they discovered more about Wes and his activities. He completed the paperwork to seize the bank accounts, successfully cutting Wes off from most of his money.

Claire knocked on his door. "How are you doing, Agent?"

Cooper nodded. "Still standing, Agent Miller. How are you doing today?"

"No complaints. I hear congratulations are in order."

Cooper laughed. "Who spilled the beans?"

"You know the Grand Rapids police department can't keep a secret!"

"Well, thank you," he said, shaking his head. "Kiely and I are very excited."

"I'm not going to hold you up. I just wanted to pop in and say hello and tell you how happy I am for you."

"I appreciate that. I was just reviewing the Neil Otis file and the information he provided."

"Have you talked to that kid?"

"No. Why?"

"I couldn't put my finger on it initially, but the more I thought I about it, I don't think he was totally honest with us about his part in all of this. It's a gut feeling. As a parent you always know when your kids are lying to your face but they think they're getting away with something. Because every kid is smarter than their parents are. I felt like he was lying through his teeth because he thinks he's smarter than the rest of us."

She took a deep breath. "Neil was more than happy to throw his mother under the bus. We heard sob stories about her mental health issues. How much he hated her boyfriend. He was a gold mine of information, no doubt. I mean, you read the report. But I wasn't happy about letting him go. We just didn't have anything to hold him on and he knew it. Personally, I think he's a powder keg waiting to explode."

"I appreciate you sharing that. Let me finish reading the file and maybe I'll drop by his home and have a chat with him myself."

"Good luck. Let me know if I can help."

Cooper gave her a nod as she exited the room. He reached for the file and flipped it open a second time. There was a picture of Neil Otis paper clipped to the inside of the folder. Although he was only eighteen years old, he looked substantially older. He had an acne problem and carried some excess weight. He was a diehard gamer, had already earned an associate degree in computer science, and worked part-time as a security guard for an industrial packing company. Cooper placed the photograph to the side but kept coming back to it as he continued to review the notes taken by his agents.

Minutes later, it clicked. He powered up his computer, then searched for an evidence folder. Inside the folder, he found the digital file he'd wanted. He played the video once and then again. After the seventh or eighth viewing he picked up his phone and dialed Claire's extension.

"Agent Winston, what's up?"

"Neil Otis participated in the kidnapping of my son. He snatched Alfie."

"Are you sure?"

"I'm positive. Pull up video #379475. It's the security tape from the school. It's him."

"I'll send a team to pick him up right now."

"I'm grabbing my vest. I'm going."

"You know you're on desk duty, right? You haven't been cleared yet."

"He snatched my son!"

"You already know the narrative. His mother made him do it."

"I'm going. I'll stay out of the way but I want to be there when they put the handcuffs on him. He terrorized my son!" Cooper's voice had risen two octaves.

"I can't approve that, Cooper. As your friend, I'm going to advise you to go home and hug your son. As your senior agent, I'm going to order you to stand down. We can't risk you jeopardizing the case. We want to see justice served. We can't risk losing him on a technicality."

Cooper threw his stapler across the room into the wall. He heaved a gust of air. "Fine," he said. "But I'm not happy about this. I'm not happy at all!"

Kiely pulled up into the driveway of her home. It felt like it had been a lifetime since she was last there. After much discussion she and Cooper had decided that she would rent her small cottage and move into the home with him and Alfie. Cooper wasn't keen on Jim Morrison coming along, having no experience with cats, but they both agreed that he might make a good companion for Alfie.

She hadn't planned to stop by the house but she had a few minutes before she was scheduled to meet Cooper. It had seemed like a good opportunity to assess all that needed to be done to prepare the house for rent. What she would take to integrate into his space, what she would leave, and what she would dole out to her siblings. She also needed to pack a second suitcase of clothes.

She didn't give much thought to the young man walking on the sidewalk in front of the property. Not until he called out to get her attention. He appeared to be young. Maybe in his late teens or early twenties. He wore a local high school's varsity sports jacket. It was ill fitting but she thought it might have more to do with the oversized sweatshirt he wore beneath it. He had bad skin, a raging case of acne across his cheeks and nose. As he moved toward her she bristled, her stance defensive, but she didn't necessarily consider him threatening. He simply appeared to be lost.

"Excuse me, ma'am? May I ask you a question, please?"

Kiely walked toward the back of her car. "Can I help you?"

"I apologize for the interruption, but my cell phone battery just died and I can't use my map feature to find Chambers Street. Do you by chance know how close I am?"

Kiely pointed right. "It's two blocks that way. You're actually very close."

"Thank you. I really appreciate that." He turned and moved to head in the direction Kiely had just pointed him to. He suddenly turned back toward her. "I'm sorry, may I ask you one more question, please?"

"Sure, what's up?"

"I really like your car. Are you happy with that model?"

Kiely narrowed her gaze ever so slightly. "My car?"

"Sorry, yeah. My father always said that if you are interested in purchasing something big, like a car, that you should ask people what they think of it when you see them driving one. He said the user

of a product can tell you more about it than a salesman. I'm actually headed to Chambers Street to see
a guy selling one. It's used. I know yours is newer
but I thought I'd ask."

Kiely nodded. She took a step closer toward the
young man. "I really like mine. I haven't had it long
but right now I have no complaints."

He nodded at her. "Thank you! I really appreciate that. You have a good day now!"

Kiely turned to head into the house when she
heard the young man suddenly rush up behind
her. Before she could respond, a heavy arm moved
around her neck and then the sharp sting of a taser
rendered her unconscious.

Cooper hated to cancel lunch with Kiely but he
was determined to see how things played out with
Neil Otis. A team had been sent to escort him into
the office and Cooper was waiting anxiously for
them to return. When she didn't answer her phone,
he sent her a quick text message.

Hate to do this but business calls. I'll explain later.
Raincheck on lunch?

Cooper had been pacing the floors, moving from
his office to the hotline call center and back. It was
taking longer than necessary to hear from the team

and he was starting to regret that he had not defied Claire and gone anyway.

Claire met him in the hallway as he was headed back toward his office. "Otis wasn't home. Two agents are going to sit on the house," she said. "They'll bring him in when he returns. Now go home. I will call you once we have him in custody."

"I think I'll wait," Cooper said. "This is personal."

"That's why you need to leave. It is personal and you're starting to be a problem."

Cooper stared her down and Claire stared back. She folded her arms across her chest and leaned against one hip.

"Fine. But please, call me."

Claire didn't bother to respond, stepping past him as she returned to her own office.

Thirty minutes later Cooper moved toward the elevators, headed home. He had managed to successfully clear off his desk, returning the last of his files to their proper place. He was trying to call Kiely for the third time when his cell phone rang, a call coming from Alfie's school. He was suddenly gripped with fear.

"Hello?"

"Hello, is this Mr. Winston?"

"Yes, it is. How may I help you?"

"Mr. Winston, this is Mrs. Glembocki. How are you, sir?"

"I'm well, thank you. Is everything okay with Alfie?"

"Yes, sir. Alfie is fine. But no one's come to pick him up. I understand you're just getting back to a routine and wondered if you had forgotten?"

"I'm sorry, my fiancée was supposed to pick him up."

"Your fiancée?"

"Kiely Colton. I added her to the approved pickup list."

"No one by that name has come to pick up Alfie."

"Thank you for calling, Mrs. Glembocki. I'm not sure what happened, but I'm on my way."

"Thank you, sir. We appreciate that."

After disconnecting the call, Cooper tried Kiely's number one more time. When it went right to voice mail, he began to worry. Kiely would never have forgotten Alfie.

# Chapter 16

**W**hen Kiely regained consciousness, she was chained to a dining room chair in her living room, and someone was puttering around in her kitchen. She tried to shake off her restraints but they wouldn't budge. She took a quick assessment of her surroundings. None of her personal possessions seemed to have been moved. A blanket rested on the floor at her feet. Her purse, cell phone, revolver and a bottle of RevitaYou rested on the coffee table. The high-definition television was on, a commercial for life insurance playing on the screen.

She turned to the clock on the wall. She knew Cooper would be looking for her. She'd been scheduled to pick up Alfie from school two hours earlier. She was certain that when she didn't arrive, he would send a search team to find her. The only thing that would delay him, she thought, was that she hadn't put visiting the house on her schedule.

"You're awake! I thought you were going to miss *Family Feud*." The young man who'd asked about her car stood in the doorway holding two TV dinners in his hands. "I really like that Steve Harvey! He's so funny!"

"Who are you?" Kiely asked. "And why are you doing this?"

"I'm sorry. Where are my manners? My name's Neil. Neil Otis."

"You're Meghan's son."

He nodded. "Steve's about to come on." He gestured with the two microwaved meals. "Would you like the Salisbury steak or the meat loaf? They both actually taste the same, if you want my opinion. Mom liked the steak better though."

"I'm not hungry. Thank you."

He shrugged. "I'll save you the steak. You can eat it later."

"Why are you doing this?"

"Let's watch Steve. We can talk later," he said, ignoring her question. He moved to the sofa and made himself comfortable, reclining back against the pillows.

Kiely struggled against her restraints a second time.

"You shouldn't do that," he said. "You might hurt yourself."

"I really need to know why you're doing this," Kiely persisted. "I don't know you."

"Yes, you do, Ms. Colton. Please don't think me a fool. I don't like that. My mother treated me like I was a fool."

"So, you know who I am?"

"I saw you at the school today. I know that you're Alfie's mom. Well, not his real mom but you act like it. You seem like a really good one, too."

"You've been watching me?"

"Of course. Well, my mother was. Sort of. You and Agent Winston. More him, than you. She really hated him."

"Is that why you're doing this? Because you hate him?"

"I don't hate anyone. Hate is not a healthy emotion."

"Then why?"

Neil seemed to ponder the question for a moment. "I don't know. I just wanted to talk to you. You had kind eyes."

"Neil, there are better ways to have a conversation with a person than kidnapping them."

"Where's your cat?" he asked, changing the subject. He pointed at the sisal-covered scratching post in the corner of the room.

"I gave her to a relative," she said.

"Your sister," he said, the statement more comment than question.

Kiely watched him keenly as he finished his meal. He lifted the paper tray to his mouth and licked it clean. When he was done, he carried it and the full tray of food back to the kitchen. "Just tell me when you're hungry," he said. "I'll heat it back up for you."

They sat together through two episodes of the *Feud*. Neil played along, pretending to be a member of the families he liked most.

"Family is very important. My mother didn't appreciate that. She treated me very badly. Mothers shouldn't treat their children badly."

"I'm sorry," Kiely said.

"Don't be. It's not your fault. My mother had emotional issues. She was very young when she had me. I don't think she knew who my father was until I was born. I think that's why she resented me. Her hatred for him is why she could never really love me."

Kiely took a breath. "I don't think that's true. Your mother told us she loved you very much."

"She told everyone that. Didn't make it true though."

He moved to the table and the bottle of Revita-You. Taking two pills from the bottle, he popped them into his mouth and washed them down with a swallow of water.

Kiely's eyes widened. "Don't take those!" she shouted.

"Why not? These are the good ones."

"The good ones?"

"Yeah, the ones that work. Mom has cases in the basement. She swore by them."

"You need to turn those over to the police."

"No," he said, sounding like he was eight and not eighteen. "These are the ones that work!" he repeated.

Kiely's frustration level was steadily rising. She knew she was in trouble, no matter how mild-mannered Neil seemed. She just wasn't sure what his endgame was. Her cell phone suddenly vibrated against the table. Neil jumped up to see who was calling, annoyed when he saw Cooper's picture on the screen.

"He calls a lot."

"He'll be looking for me, Neil. A lot of people will be looking for me."

"No, they won't. I've been texting them. He thinks you're helping your sister with a problem. Your sister thinks you're in a meeting and can't talk. No one is missing you."

"My son is missing me."

Neil slammed a heavy fist against the table. He rose from his seat and stormed back into the kitchen. Minutes later, when he returned, so had his mild-mannered mood.

"I don't want you to talk about him."

"Why? He's just a baby!"

Neil winced, her words apparently off putting to him. "My mother kept saying that. He's a baby! Watch the baby! Be nice to the baby! Mother wanted to keep him. But I couldn't let her do that. I had to protect him."

"You need to let me go, Neil. This is ridiculous! You can't keep me hostage here forever."

"It's not forever."

"Then for how long?"

"You really need to eat," Neil said. He moved to the back of the sofa, rummaging on the floor. When he stood, he held a gas can in his hands and began to splash gasoline on the furniture and floor.

Kiely's eyes widened. "What are you doing? Why are you doing that?"

"Because you're a good mom now. I don't want you to be a bad mother. You'll go bad. All of you go bad. I have to stop you before that happens. I have to do it for the children."

Alfie had finally cried himself to sleep. He'd been devastated when Kiely hadn't picked him up. When she hadn't arrived by dinner, he'd been beside himself. It had taken Cooper forever to calm him down. Although Kiely hadn't answered Cooper's calls, she had texted him. Multiple times. She'd been apologetic about not showing to pick up Alfie, claiming an emergency with her sister was holding her up. But now his concern had increased tenfold. Something wasn't right and he regretted not following his first instinct.

Reaching for his cell phone, he read through the text messages a second time. Most of the responses were short and sweet. But short and sweet didn't feel like Kiely. He sent one last message.

Should we invite the deer to the wedding?

As he waited for her to respond, he paced the floor. He needed to find her. And something in his gut told him he needed to find her quick.

A reply message came back promptly.

I'd rather invite the kangaroos!

Cooper placed three phone calls. The first was to the FBI offices. The second call was to Lieutenant McKellar and the third was to Riley Colton.

"We're pinging her phone now to see if we can get a location on her. Can you check if any of your sisters have heard from her, please?" Cooper said.

"I'll call them now and I'll call you right back. Do you have any idea what's happened to her?"

"Not a clue," Cooper answered.

Cooper had just called the teenager down the

street to come sit with Alfie when his phone rang, Claire on the other end.

"Hey, did they update you?" Cooper questioned.

"Yes," his friend answered. "But you're not going to believe this," she said. "We just got a DNA hit on three murders. The agency hadn't wanted to say they were the work of a serial killer, but the similarities in each case can't be ignored. Three young mothers with small children, all kidnapped, each burned alive in their homes. The last murder occurred one year ago."

"Why are you telling me this? I've never worked any of those cases."

"Because that DNA is the same as Neil Otis's. He's a perfect match and we still haven't been able to find him."

Something dark pitched through the pit of Cooper's stomach. He suddenly felt like the tuna fish sandwich he'd eaten for dinner might come back up. Pieces of a puzzle were falling into place through no effort of his and he wasn't liking the picture coming forward.

"And all the murders occurred in the victims' homes?" he asked.

"That's correct."

Panic swept through Cooper like a storm wind. He shouted into the receiver. "I need a team sent to Kiely Colton's house now! She's missing and if Neil

Otis is your serial killer then she may be your next victim. I think he might have her there!"

The smell of gasoline was thick through the air. Kiely found it revolting. It was turning her stomach and giving her a vicious headache. Neil seemed oblivious to it as he sat watching an episode of *Thundercats*. He had abandoned all efforts at conversation, ignoring Kiely's admonishments for him to talk to her.

When the cartoon was over, he asked her one last time, if she wanted something to eat. "I can heat up your TV dinner if you're hungry. You really should have one last meal. All the others ate their last meal."

"The others? You've done this before, Neil?"

"Of course! There are so many children that need to be saved."

Kiely closed her eyes, the significance of what he intended feeling like a gut punch. She couldn't begin to fathom how she had come to be in this place. Or how Neil had become the way he was. A tear ran down her cheek. All she wanted was to get back to Cooper and Alfie.

"Was there anyone in your life who you loved, Neil, who you miss now?"

Neil's expression was cutting. "No," he said matter-of-factly. "Not really."

"Did you love your mother?"

"When I was small. Like your son's age. And I tried to be really good so that she would love me, but it never worked."

"Well, Alfie loves me, Neil. Alfie will miss me. If you do this, you are going to break his heart. You won't be saving him, you'll be hurting him."

Neil looked at her. "This hurt will go away and soon he won't even remember you. And when he does, all he'll remember is what a good mother you were. He'll never have to remember you turning on him. You really should thank me."

Kiely begged. "Please! Don't do this."

Neil moved to her side and patted her hand. "I can give you something if it'll make it easier. Mom had tranquilizers and pain pills stashed away. All kinds of stuff."

"Go to hell!" Kiely snapped.

Neil bristled. "See, it never fails," he shouted. "All of you go bad! Before you know it you'll be calling Alfie bad names and hitting him and you'll hurt his feelings and…" He became choked up, fighting not to cry. He gasped for air, then just like that collected himself.

"It's time!" he exclaimed, his singsong tone disconcerting.

"What do you mean? What are you going to do? Please don't do this, Neil! Please!"

Despite her best efforts to remain calm, panic had begun to set in. Kiely shook the chains harder, desperate to release herself. Panic suddenly became rage. Neil had disappeared to the second floor of her home, a second gasoline can in his hands. He rested the container at the bottom of the steps and then he moved to turn the television volume up higher.

He lit one match and then the entire book, tossing both to the floor behind the sofa. Flames suddenly shot skyward. He moved to Kiely's side one last time.

"It was very nice talking with you, Ms. Colton," he said, and then he walked calmly out the front door.

## Chapter 17

Cooper arrived at Kiely's house seconds after Claire and her team had descended on the property. The fire department was already on-site, fighting the barrage of flames that lit up the late-night sky. His heart dropped into the pit of his stomach and he raced toward the house screaming Kiely's name.

Someone from the fire department grabbed him by the shoulders and swung him back around, refusing to let him pass. There was a struggle of wills as the fireman ducked a punch he threw, Cooper determined to get inside the home.

Claire suddenly grabbed his arm, pulling at his attention. "Cooper, Kiely's okay! Kiely's fine!" she shouted above the noise of his screams.

Claire pointed to the EMS vehicle. "She suffered some smoke inhalation, but she's fine."

Tears were streaming down Cooper's face. He grabbed Claire and hugged her before tearing across the yard to the ambulance. Kiely lay on a gurney inside, an oxygen mask over her face. He jumped into the back of the vehicle and when she saw him, she ripped the mask off. Sitting upright Kiely stretched her arms out and clung tightly to him.

Cooper kissed her cheeks, her forehead, her nose, her lips. Kisses rained down on every square inch of her face and he refused to let her go until his nerves had calmed, his heart beating normally again.

"Are you okay? Did he hurt you?" Cooper questioned.

"I'm fine. Really. I'm okay."

"Her vitals are good," the technician said. "But we should transport her to the hospital to be examined."

"That's not necessary," Kiely said. "I feel fine. I'm not going to the hospital." She threw her legs over the side of the gurney and went to stand but felt light-headed and sat back down.

"You're going, Kiely."

"I really don't want to. It's not necessary."

"I'll meet you there," Cooper said, his tone commanding. "Let a doctor clear you and then we can go home to Alfie."

"Is he okay?"

"Pissed that you weren't in the kiss and go lane this afternoon."

"My poor baby!"

"He'll be very happy to see you."

Kiely hugged him one more time. She was shaking slightly, hoping no one noticed. But Cooper noticed and he was suddenly angry that someone had tried to hurt her. He kissed her cheek. "I'll be right behind you," he said.

Jumping out of the ambulance, he watched until it pulled off, sirens screaming. He turned, searching out Agent Miller. Claire stood by a government-issued vehicle, debriefing one of her agents. Spying Cooper, she met him halfway as he moved in her direction.

"Please, tell me we did not lose this monster."

"Nope, we got him." She pointed to the back seat of a police patrol car. Neil Otis was leaning against the window peering out at the burning house. He looked lost and completely enamored with the flames that were being extinguished. "He'd barely gotten out the front door when we took him down. Kiely was chained to a chair in the front room and two of our agents went in and carried her out."

"I owe them my gratitude."

"Thank them by getting Kiely and going home and please don't come back until you have medical clearance from an agency doctor. Spend some time with your family, *not* working. Is that clear, Agent?"

"Have a good night, Claire. And thank you!" He turned, hurrying back to his car.

Claire called his name.

"Yes?"

"Good work, Agent Winston!"

Kiely was so ready to be done with the emergency room that she was sitting in the waiting room when Cooper arrived.

"What took you so long?"

"Why are you out here?"

"Do you always answer a question with a question?"

"Depends upon the question?"

"Do you love me?"

"Forever and always." Cooper captured her lips with his own. The kiss was tender and heated. When he finally let her go, he asked, "Have you been officially released?"

"If I say yes will you believe me?"

He chuckled. "And you give me a hard time."

Grabbing her hand, they made their way to the car and then home. Kiely called her brother to let him know she was safe and sound so that her family wouldn't be worrying about her. After a quick lecture, she was ready to be done with retelling what had happened to her.

"I feel sorry for him," Kiely said. "He's got serious issues."

"He's a psychopath."

"He thinks he's helping children."

"Well, thankfully he will never be able to hurt anyone else again."

Kiely sighed. She didn't have the energy to tell Cooper she was tired of this conversation. She wasn't much interested in solving anyone else's problems or putting herself in the path of danger. The only thing she wanted was to crawl into bed and forget that anything had happened. To ignore that Neil had disturbed her peace and left her feeling battered. She needed time to let it all go so that she could feel like herself again and not be afraid.

"Can we talk about this some other time?" she asked.

Cooper nodded. "Of course. Anything you want. You look tired."

"I just want to go to bed and I want you to just hold me."

He nodded again. "Baby, you can have anything you want."

The first thing Kiely did when they got back to Cooper's house was peek in on Alfie. He was sleeping soundly, his thumb in his mouth and his favorite blue blanket clutched in his fist. She brushed the hair off his forehead and leaned to give him a kiss.

She knew she smelled like smoke and she headed straight for a hot shower. She was grateful for Cooper giving her time alone to decompress and process everything that had happened. For a while there she didn't think there was enough soap and water or shampoo and conditioner to help her get the smell of fear off of her. She'd had many close calls over the years, but there had been something about this one that felt like dead weight on her shoulders, refusing to let go.

By the time Kiely had finished in the bathroom, Cooper was already showered and in bed. He'd used the bathroom in the spare bedroom, wanting her to take as much time as she needed. He understood that what she had just experienced was traumatizing and even the strongest person would have difficulties getting past it all.

She pulled a T-shirt from his top drawer and pulled it over her head. She slid into bed beside him and Cooper curled his body around hers. The nearness of him, the sound of his breathing, brought her joy that could not be verbalized. It just made her feel like all was well in the world. Back in Cooper's arms, Kiely felt like she'd found her way back home. The lights were on, a fire was burning in the fireplace and the smell of baking cookies filled the air.

"I love you," Kiely whispered. "I love you so much."

Cooper squeezed her gently. He threw his leg over hers and tightened the hold he had on her. He pressed a damp kiss against the back of her neck.

"Twenty questions," Kiely said. "What one place would you live if you didn't live in Grand Rapids?"

"Hawaii!"

"I like Hawaii! I could live there."

Cooper smiled. "Favorite flower?"

"Hydrangea. Favorite president?"

"Good question! I'd say... Jimmy Carter."

"Good answer!"

Cooper kept it going. "Last book you read."

"It was a mystery. *City of Saviors* by Rachel Howzell Hall."

"Not an author I know. Was it good?"

"I really liked it. Morning person or night person."

"Morning person."

"I'm more of a night person but I make it work when I have to."

Cooper hesitated, looking like he wasn't sure what to ask next.

"It's your turn," Kiely said to coax him along.

"Are you really okay, Kiely?"

She suddenly choked back a sob. "No," she said softly. "No, I'm not. But I will be. I'm home and I'm going to be just fine."

Cooper held her close for the rest of the night. He kneaded her shoulders and stroked her back. When she jumped in her sleep he whispered in her ear to soothe her. He would have done anything to ensure she was well.

\* \* \*

Kiely woke the next morning to Alfie tapping her face with the palm of his hand. Her mouth lifted in a warm smile but she didn't open her eyes. He tapped her a second time. She opened one eye and closed it again. His giggles were music to her ears and Alfie was giggling merrily.

He leaned to kiss her cheek. "Hi, Ki-Ki! You sleep?"

Kiely reached out to give him a tickle and Alfie erupted in laughter. "Do again! Do again!" he exclaimed, not wanting her to stop.

When Cooper came to check on the two of them they were cuddled together watching cartoons.

"Hey, buddy," Cooper said, "are you ready to go to school today?"

"No, Alfie stay home wit' Ki-Ki. No go school!"

"I propose we have family day," Kiely said.

"Family day? What's that?" Cooper asked.

"Daddy and Alfie and Kiely stay home together all day in bed watching cartoons."

"Yeah! Family day!" Alfie said excitedly.

Cooper laughed. "Does that mean we get to stay in our pajamas all day?"

"Pajamas all day, and we pop popcorn, and play games!" Kiely said excitedly. "Maybe we'll even have a dance party!"

"And cartoons!" Alfie added.

Kiely gave the boy a little squeeze and another tickle.

"Well," Cooper said, "what would you two like to eat for breakfast?"

"I propose cereal with the marshmallows in it and we eat it right out of the box."

Alfie threw up his hands in agreement. "Cereal!"

"I'll have coffee with mine. Can I tempt you with a cup?"

"Alfie want milk," the little boy said firmly. "Just milk."

Kiely said, "One milk and one coffee would be appreciated. Thank you."

Breakfast was a big hit with Alfie, even with the spilled milk and cereal in the bed. They played games, watched cartoons, and spent the entire morning and afternoon together. Only once did Cooper try to answer his cell phone. After the dirty looks his son and Kiely gave him, he turned the device off and focused solely on the two of them.

Kiely made grilled cheese sandwiches, tomato soup and popped popcorn for lunch. Before putting Alfie down for a nap, the couple sat him down to talk about their plans.

"Alfie, how would you like Kiely to be your mommy?" Cooper questioned.

"Alfie mommy in hea-ben."

"Yes, she is. Your mommy Sara is in heaven," Cooper said. "But Kiely would like to be your *bonus* mommy, and Daddy *wants* Kiely to do that. How do you feel about that?"

"Alfie *lub* Ki-Ki!"

"So, you want to keep her?"

"Ki-Ki mine!"

"Yes, I am!" Kiely said.

Alfie jumped from his chair and took off running. They could hear him laughing in the other room.

"Why did I think having a serious conversation with a two-year-old was going to be easy?" Cooper said.

"It was."

"Are you sure? Because I'm not sure he got it."

Kiely smiled. "Trust me, he got it."

Minutes later Alfie came tearing back into the room with his stuffed rabbit. He shoved the toy in Kiely's direction. "Dis babbitt!"

"Hello, rabbit!"

He looked into the rabbit's face, poking it in the eyes. He climbed into Kiely's lap. "You Alfie mommy!"

"Yes, I am!"

"Alfie *lub* you Ki-Ki!" He wrapped his little arms around Kiely's neck and hugged her.

Kiely met the look Cooper was giving her. She grinned. "Told you!"

Family day lasted three whole days. By day four Alfie was excited to go back to school to play with his friends. Cooper headed to the office so Claire could yell at him about being there, and Kiely began to deal with the insurance company over the demise of her home and the loss of her property.

Someone from Cooper's office had retrieved her new car, depositing it in the empty parking space. She had driven by her house to assess the damage, but once she turned on the street she hadn't been able to stop. Passing by had been all she could manage and Cooper had agreed that had been more than enough. There was nothing inside that couldn't be replaced.

After making the turn at the corner Kiely headed to her brother's. Riley had called a meeting of Colton Investigations, insisting they all needed to be there. She knew he wanted to assess where they were with Brody's case, but it was also about the Colton siblings laying eyes on each other with everything that had been happening.

Traffic was light which made the ride easy and it took no time at all for Kiely to get to Grand Avenue, near the center of the historic Heritage Hill neighborhood. Riley lived in the family home where they'd grown up. The siblings had inherited the house after their parents' tragic deaths and operated Colton Investigations out of the rooms on the first floor. Deciding to make the locale CI headquarters had just made sense.

She pulled into the driveway and eased her car

behind the house. Parking the vehicle behind Pippa's luxury sedan, she realized she wasn't the last to arrive. Their sister Vikki wasn't there yet either. That would take some of the heat off her when she walked in. Riley hated when they weren't on time.

She didn't bother to knock, throwing the door open and heading inside. Riley and Griffin were sitting at the kitchen table noshing on containers of Chinese food. Riley's German Shepherd, Pal, sat between them, her large head bobbing back and forth as she hoped one or the other would drop something to the hardwood floor.

"Hey," she said, greeting her brothers.

She rubbed Pal's head and the dog licked her hand in greeting.

Riley dropped the egg roll between his fingers onto his plate. He reached for a napkin. "I didn't know if you were coming. You never answered my text message. I was starting to worry."

Kiely shrugged. "Sorry about that. I had a lot going on."

"Cooper told us what happened and we saw the house."

She nodded. "It's totaled. I've lost everything, but I've gained far more than I lost." She leaned to give Griffin a hug. "How are you?"

"Better than you apparently."

Kiely smiled. "If we can talk later, I need a favor.

Cooper and I need an adoption attorney. I want to legally adopt his son Alfie."

Griffin was about to take a bite of his food, his fork stalling in midair. "I've clearly missed out on a lot!" he said, a hint of attitude in his tone.

"Not really," she said. "And if you have, I'm excited to catch you up."

He nodded. "You know I'll do whatever I can. Just let me know when you two want to schedule an appointment to meet."

Kiely leaned to kiss his cheek. "Where's everyone?"

"The girls are in the dining room. Are you hungry?" Riley said. "There's plenty of food. Just grab a paper plate and help yourself."

"I will," she said. "Let me go say hi to everyone first."

"Make it quick! Meeting starts in ten." Riley pulled his egg roll back to his mouth.

Kiely maneuvered her way through the home. As she entered the main area, Ashanti Silver, her favorite tech guru, jumped from her seat to greet her. Ashanti was one of her brother's first hires. Gorgeous, super smart and a wiz with a computer, she could back door her way past anyone's firewall and never be detected. She had helped Kiely get out of many situations, some business and some personal.

The woman threw her arms around Kiely in a bear hug. "Oh, my God! You're alive!"

Kiely laughed. "No one's killed me off yet! How are you?"

"I've got my heels and my health so I have no complaints," she said as she showed off the six-inch stilettos she was wearing. She tossed her long braids over her shoulder. "More importantly, I want to see that ring," she said as she waved her fingers at Kiely.

Kiely held out her hand. The two-carat diamond in the antique setting flattered her fingers.

"It's beautiful!" Ashanti hugged her a second time. "I'm so excited for you. Now, do you need me to run a background check on him?" she asked.

Kiely laughed. "I'm good. I appreciate you offering though."

"If you need me, just ask."

Kiely continued into the dining conference room. Pippa and Sadie sat at the oversized table thumbing through wedding gown magazines. Both women stood up to hug her.

"Why haven't you called anyone?" Pippa admonished. "I've left a dozen messages for you."

Kiely shrugged. "I needed some time."

"You're lucky Cooper's so good about keeping us all updated," Sadie quipped.

"You talked to Cooper?"

"We didn't talk to you!"

Kiely smiled. She would have to thank him later for looking out for her, she thought.

"Are you hungry?" Pippa asked. "I'll make you a plate if you want me to?"

Kiely shook her head. "I might get something after the meeting. I'm good for now."

Her sister tapped the empty seat beside her. "Sit down."

"We've taken up a donation for you," Sadie said.

"What kind of donation?"

"We all cleaned out our closets to collect some clothes for you. There are three large bags in the trunk of my car," Pippa interjected. "It should tide you over until you can start rebuilding your wardrobe."

Kiely laughed. "I hadn't even thought about it. I've spent the last three days in my pajamas."

"I bet that was cute," Sadie giggled.

"Cooper liked it," Kiely said with a smirk.

The conversation was interrupted when the brothers moved into the room. Riley took the seat at the head of the table. "Has anyone heard from Vikki?"

Gazes shifted back and forth and heads shook from side to side.

"I guess we'll start without her." Riley cleared his throat. "I think it's safe to say we are no farther along with this case than we were before. Still nothing solid on a location for Wes Matthews or Landon Street."

Kiely shared what she and Cooper had learned

from Neil Otis. "Cooper has cut off much of Wes's bank access. Unless he has accounts that haven't been found yet, he'll be hurting for money sooner than later. That might be to our advantage. Cooper's office is still running down the leads Neil gave them."

"I feel like we're looking for a needle in a haystack," Pippa said. "Those two are cagey as hell!"

Kiely shot Sadie a quick look. "Cooper's also trying to find a connection between Matthews and Tate Greer. It looks like most of the victims who financed their investments in RevitaYou were referred to Capital X with guarantees of approved financing."

Riley nodded. "We'll see what we can find out on our end."

"Has anyone spoke to Brody recently?" Griffin asked. He looked directly at Pippa.

She shook her head. "Not a word. I don't know if we should be worried or not."

Everyone at the table went quiet, thinking about their surrogate brother and his predicament. The moment was suddenly interrupted when Vikki rushed into the room.

"Hello! Hello! Hello!" She moved around the table pressing her cheek to everyone else's.

"You're late," Riley admonished.

"And I can't stay. I just came for a quick lunch,"

she said. "We've had another RevitaYou death. A woman named Teri Emerson."

Riley cussed.

"Is she military?" Kiely questioned.

Vikki was a JAG paralegal for the U.S. Armed Forces assigned to Fort Rapids.

"Military wife," she answered. "Her husband is an army captain and he's on a rampage. He's looking for Landon Street and has vowed to kill him on sight. I've been assigned to investigate his threats. He's highly decorated and about to retire. I'm trying to keep this from blowing up even more."

"Understood," Riley said. "Do what you have to do."

"Is there anything I need to know, before I run out of here?" Vikki asked.

Riley threw up his hands in frustration. "No, there really isn't much we have to share."

Vikki nodded. She turned her attention toward Kiely. "Call me, please, and let me know what's going on with you. In fact, call and update me, if there is anything that comes out here that I need to know, too, please."

She gave her sister a hug, also grabbing her hand to look at her engagement ring. "Clearly, he has good taste!"

Laughter rang around the table as Victoria made her exit. She called out over her shoulder, "I'm tak-

ing an egg roll and the rest of the beef and peppers!
I hope nobody wanted it."

Griffin laughed. "I guess if they did, it's too late."

# Chapter 18

Cooper stood in front of the burned-out shell that was once her home, waiting for her. While she had met with her siblings, he had taken the meeting with the insurance agent. She couldn't begin to tell him how much she appreciated his efforts. As she moved to his side, she felt herself begin to shake. She realized that even if the home had not burned, that returning to it would not have been easy.

Cooper immediately wrapped her in his arms and kissed her forehead. Kiely took a deep breath and held it for a brief moment before blowing it out slowly.

"How did your meeting go?" Cooper asked.

"It went really well," Kiely responded. And it

had. After Vikki had made her exit, Kiely and her siblings had a conversation about her taking a step back from the business. She wanted to continue working on Brody's case until it was resolved, but didn't want to take on anything new. Her family had been super supportive. Riley, in particular, had let her know he would be there for her however she needed him to be. He promised not to call on her until she was ready.

"What did the insurance agent have to say?"

"Well, you won't be renting it anytime soon."

Kiely laughed. "So the agent has jokes like you have jokes."

"You had full coverage, so you have nothing to worry about. They'll be paying you fair market value for the house and for the land. When you're ready you can decide whether or not you want to rebuild or sell."

"I'm glad I don't have to make a decision anytime soon."

"Not until you're ready." He kissed her again.

"We have an hour before we have to pick up Alfie. Is there anything special you'd like to do?" He arched his eyebrows and gave her a look.

Kiely laughed. "Aren't you fresh!"

"We've never done an afternoon quickie."

"We might have to do that."

Cooper reached for her hand and entwined her fingers between his own.

"Twenty questions?"

"Ask away."

"Chicken or beef?"

"Beef, preferably grass fed. Birth control?"

Cooper looked confused. "Birth control?"

"Stop or keep taking it," she said teasingly.

He grinned. "Interesting! Stop or keep taking it? Hmm? I'd be happy either way. As long as you're happy with whatever decision you make for your body."

Kiely smiled and lifted her chin to reach his lips. She kissed him slowly, allowing her mouth to glide sweetly over his.

"Favorite girl names?"

"Good question! Emily, Allison and Grace are at the top of my list."

"I love Grace."

"Shaved or unshaved?"

"Are we talking a specific body part or body parts in general?" Cooper questioned.

Kiely shrugged her shoulders, a sly look on her face.

"Some parts shaved and some parts not shaved," he answered.

Kiely laughed and Cooper laughed with her. Joy blew with a quiet breeze that billowed around them. The temperature was beginning to drop and there was just a hint of a chill in the air. Kiely pressed herself against him and kissed his lips one more time.

"I have tinted windows," she said. "You ever get a quickie in the back seat of a new car?"

Cooper grinned. "No, but I think I'm about to."

Kiely turned and headed toward her new vehicle. Her hips swayed seductively from side to side. Cooper looked around quickly to see who might be watching and then he hurried after her. She climbed into the back seat and he followed. As he closed and locked the door, Kiely's delightful laugh danced sweetly with his.

\* \* \* \* \*

*Don't miss the previous volumes in
the Colton 911: Grand Rapids series:*

Colton 911: Family Defender
*by Tara Taylor Quinn*
Colton 911: Suspect Under Siege
*by Jane Godman*
Colton 911: Detective on Call
*by Regan Black*

*Available now from
Harlequin Romantic Suspense*

*And don't miss the thrilling next installment*

Colton 911: In Hot Pursuit
*by Geri Krotow*
*Available in November 2020!*

*When a lead points security agency Rocky Mountain
Justice in the direction of a posh resort in the hunt for a
serial killer, operative and single dad Liam Alexander
and child psychologist Holly Jacobs work together to
hunt the huntress, eventually posing as a family to trap
their prey. But as their plan backfires, Liam will do
anything to save his child—and the woman he loves.*

*Read on for a sneak preview of
the next book in the Wyoming Nights miniseries,*
Agent's Mountain Rescue,
*by Jennifer D. Bokal.*

"Look at us, we're quite the mismatched pair. Still,
we make a decent team." Reaching for her hand, Liam
stared at their joined fingers. "Plus," he added, "you're
pretty easy to talk to and to trust. I don't do either of
those things easily, but then I think you've figured that
out already. I like that about you, Holly."

She inched closer, her breath caressing his cheek.
"You're not so bad yourself."

He smiled a little. "That's better than you turning me
down."

She licked her lips. Looking away, Holly stared at
something just beyond Liam's shoulder. "I don't want to
complicate things."

"I understand," he said, even though he didn't. He wanted her. She wanted him. It all seemed pretty simple and straightforward. "I'm not going to pressure you into anything here."

"Do you really understand?" she asked. "Because I'm not sure that I know what's going on myself."

"You have your life plan. You need money to keep your school open. A relationship is a complication. Besides, you could be leaving town, which means us getting involved could be difficult for Sophie."

Holly touched her fingertips to his lips, silencing him. "If I can't get the money to keep Saplings, then I'll definitely have to leave Pleasant Pines," she said. "You said it yourself—I might not be around much longer."

"Now I'm really confused. What are you saying?"

"Kiss me," she whispered.

It was all the invitation he needed.

*Don't miss*
Agent's Mountain Rescue *by Jennifer D. Bokal,*
*available November 2020 wherever*
*Harlequin Romantic Suspense*
*books and ebooks are sold.*

Harlequin.com

HRSEXP1020